HER MAIL ORDER MISCONCEPTION

LONDON JAMES

long
VALLEY
PRESS

ONE

ELSA

And all the world is your stage.

Elsa didn't know how often her uncle had said those words to her. A hundred. A thousand. A hundred thousand.

In the end, she didn't think it mattered. It wasn't the number of times he said it that mattered; it was when he said it, which was right after she ended her last song, and the show was over. It was like a blanket that a child carried, something always there and always could calm her down after the excitement of the bright lights shining upon her as she belted out the different melodies for the crowd.

There was nothing more thrilling than a standing ovation, and each night after receiving one, Uncle Clancy would hug her and whisper those words.

Just as he did tonight.

"Thank you, Uncle Clancy," she whispered back.

"I'll wait for you in my office. There are a few dresses for you to pick from for tonight."

A slight groan left her lips, and she cocked her head to the side. "Must we go to the Hideaway Club after the show? I'm so tired, and I would like to go home for the rest of the evening."

"Of course, we have to go to the club. Everyone is expecting you to show up. It's what you always do after a performance. It's expected of you."

"But I'm exhausted."

"It doesn't matter, Elsa. That is your job as a performer. You know this."

"How long do I have to stay? Can I show my face for a few minutes, then leave?"

"You know you can't just spend minutes there. We have a meeting with Mr. Tillman tonight. He's meeting us in one of the lounge rooms, and he wishes to discuss a roadshow that will take you to some of the biggest cities in the country,"

"I don't know if I want to do that roadshow."

"For heaven's sakes, why not?"

"Because the last one was a bit too much for me. Eight weeks on the road. Eight weeks away from home. I don't want to do another one. I have more than enough money to last me a while. I don't need to do another one so soon. Can't it just wait until next year?"

"No, Elsa. It can't. Now go, change. I'll be waiting in my office."

Before Elsa could protest any further, Uncle Clancy walked off toward his office, leaving her standing alone in the hallway. She didn't want to think about how the rest of the evening would play out. There was a time she liked the Hideaway Club and going there after a show. So many men flattered her with their applause and attention upon her arrival, offering to buy her drinks—which she never would consume, but at least the thought was nice.

Of course, she didn't just go for the men. She wasn't that type of woman. But it was just a part of the nightlife that continued to give her the same butterflies as she had on stage. A lavish scene, one full of wealth, fancy clothes, expensive jewelry, and the most delicious appetizers she'd ever tasted. Lobster, crab, even scallops—delicacies she never enjoyed as a child, growing up in a modest family who had little money. Not that she held little regard for her parents. She loved them so much and missed them every day. There were so many times after their accident that she would lie in bed at night, telling God if he'd bring them back, she would hand over every penny in her bank account.

It never worked, however.

God didn't make bargains like that.

Thinking about the club tonight, though, was different. She didn't want to go, didn't want to see anyone or talk to anyone. She just wanted to go home, curl up in her bed with a cup of tea and read. It'd been forever since she'd enjoyed a night like that, and as she walked down the hallway toward her dressing room, it was the kind of night she longed for so badly, she could taste it.

"Darn, Uncle Clancy, for making me go to the club tonight," she whispered to herself as she opened the door. She didn't like cursing his name, but at that moment, it seemed warranted.

Shutting the door behind her, she blew out a breath and looked around her dressing room. Her home away from home, as she often thought about it, she both loved the space and hated it, loved it for it was her own, hated it because it never seemed like the great escape she wanted it to feel like. Although she supposed that wasn't exactly the room's fault.

At least not entirely.

Still, something about it never felt right but always felt a little off. No matter how many paintings she hung on the walls or how many vases of flowers she brought in and set in every available inch she could, or no matter how many times she changed out the furniture. It just was off.

Ignoring the way she wanted to change everything about it

for the one-hundredth time, she made her way over to the sofa in the corner, studying the few dresses that were draped over the back—dresses Uncle Clancy had laid out for her to choose from to wear tonight at the club. Looking down upon them, she knew which one he would want her to wear—the red one—and she thought of grabbing it and tossing it on the floor to get it dirty.

Oh, how he would be furious, she thought to herself.

Still, the thought amused her, and she traced her fingers over the red material a little longer as she smiled.

"Furious indeed," she whispered.

As she bent down to grab it, a hand reached around and covered her mouth. She screamed, but the sound was muffled, and as she tried to spin around to face the person behind her, an arm wrapped around her shoulders. Whoever had her drew her body into theirs, holding her tight while she struggled against the force trying to contain and hold her prisoner.

She screamed again.

And again.

And again until she resorted to thrashing in hopes that she could break free. Finally, the person spun her around, releasing his grip. As she glimpsed at the sight of a masked man, he lifted his hand and slapped her across the face. Her skin stung, and the force knocked her off balance. She stumbled a few steps, nearly falling to the ground. The man lunged for her again, slapping her a second and third time. Each time was harder than the last, and she fell. She struggled to get up, crawling on the floor toward the door. She only managed a few feet when the man climbed over her, using his weight to pin her to the ground. He covered her face again and brandished a knife. The blade glinted in the light of the sconces on the dressing room's walls. Sconces she had shipped from New York because she liked the look and style.

Her heart thumped, and she fought against his crushing

weight. Her life flashed before her eyes—all her performances, the cheering crowd, the news of her parent's accident, and lastly, their faces looking upon her and smiling. It was as though she was about to go to Heaven and see them again.

No. I'm not, she thought to herself. I'm fighting back.

She bit down on the palm of the man's hand. He let out a yelp and removed it from her mouth, slapping her again. Her mind went fuzzy, and her vision blurred. She didn't know how many more hits she could stand, but she continued to jerk her body to break free. The man struggled against her movement, failing to grab her wrist and pin it to the floor. She rolled over, kicking her legs. Her foot hit the side of his face, and the heel of her shoe caught his ear. He cried out, grabbing the side of his head for a moment. It was an advantage she needed and one that she used. She kicked him again and again until he lost control over her and fell off her, dropping the knife.

She crawled toward it, grabbing it before he could recover it himself, and she pointed it at him for a moment before lunging toward him. She sliced at the air, and as he lifted his hand to block her advancement, the blade cut the palm of his hand. Blood spattered, and he backed away from her, holding his hand. She ran at him again, growling. He ducked and moved around her, fleeing the dressing room before escaping down the hallway. She dropped to her knees, crying out and screaming for Uncle Clancy.

~

"Mr. Bates, the sheriff is here." Jerry, the door manager of the theater, popped his head inside the dressing room door as he hooked his thumb over his shoulder.

"Thank you, Jerry. You can send him on back to the dressing room." Uncle Clancy sat on the sofa next to Elsa, glancing at the doorman before his gaze returned to his niece. "The sheriff is going to ask you a bunch of questions. I know you might not wish to answer them, but you have to. Do you understand me?"

She nodded. Unable to speak, she just sat staring at the floor where she'd been attacked moments ago. The whole scene replayed in her mind, and her body trembled.

"Let me get you a blanket." Uncle Clancy stood and made his way over to the vanity, fetching the blanket on the back of her chair. The one she used while getting ready to keep warm. The heating was never up to par in the theater, and tonight had been no different. He laid it over her shoulders, wrapping it tight before rubbing his hands up and down her arms. "When he's done with the questioning, I'll take you home. All right?"

She nodded again.

Uncle Clancy watched her before heaving a sigh and sitting back down on the couch. They waited for a moment until the sheriff arrived, and Uncle Clancy stood to greet him.

"Thank you for coming so quickly."

"Of course. How is Miss Crestwood?"

"She's in shock, I think. She hasn't said much since it happened. I don't know if she can give you the information you need. I was thinking tomorrow might be a better time to question her."

The sheriff shook his head. "It's better to get the details right after it happens when everything is fresh in their minds. Don't worry, Mr. Bates. I know how to handle these types of things." Before Uncle Clancy could argue any further, the sheriff made his way over to the sofa and knelt in front of Elsa.

"Good evening, ma'am. I know you are probably not up to answering my questions, but I need you to try. Can you do that for me?"

She blinked at him while his words registered in her mind, then she nodded.

"Do you know who the man was who attacked you?"

She shook her head.

"You didn't get any glimpse of anything that could be used to describe him?"

She shook her head again.

"Maybe this isn't the time for all this." Uncle Clancy stepped forward. He ran his hands through his hair as he started to pace in front of them.

"Mr. Bates, please. Let me do my job."

As Uncle Clancy turned away from the sheriff, Rick, his right-hand man, came darting through the door. With his hands shoved in his pockets, his lungs heaved, and he glanced all around the room. His eyes widened. "What did I miss? What happened?"

"Elsa was attacked." Clancy's words made Elsa cringe. It was as though hearing them made the memories more real.

While she could try to tell herself that it'd been a dream, that it didn't happen and she only just thought that it did, hearing someone else say it out loud . . . she couldn't pretend her way out of that.

"Do you know who it was?" Rick asked.

Uncle Clancy shook his head. "She doesn't know."

The two of them continued to start at one another while the sheriff adjusted his balance in front of her. "Miss Crestwood? Is there anything at all you can tell me? How tall was he? What was the color of his hair? His eyes? Was he thin? Was he a heavier set? What was he wearing? Anything at all? It's essential that you try to remember, Miss Crestwood."

The sheriff inched closer to her, and as she felt the warmth of his body, her heart thumped. She scooted away from him, retreating to the other end of the sofa. Her breaths quickened.

Rick and Uncle Clancy moved toward the sheriff, and as Rick grabbed him with one hand, the sheriff jerked and spun, ripping Rick's other hand from inside his pocket. Rick yelped and hissed, revealing a bandage around his hand.

"What happened to you?" the sheriff asked.

"I slammed it in the door while I was rushing here. It's nothing."

Elsa glanced up, and the bandage caught her breath. It was the same hand—the right one—that she'd cut on the man who attacked her. She'd never noticed Rick's build before, but as he stood next to the sheriff, she studied his height and weight until she saw it was the same as the man's frame who attacked her.

Why would Rick attack her?

Weakness poured through her body, and she trembled.

What was going on? What would cause either of them . . .

No, she couldn't think about the reasons.

She needed to get out of the theater.

Needed to get away from everyone.

And needed to go home.

She stood and made her way across the dressing room, fetching the suitcase she'd brought with her that night. It wasn't much, just a few changes of clothes—something she brought with her every night just in case she needed it.

"What are you doing?" Uncle Clancy asked.

"I need to go home."

"All right. I can have Rick bring the carriage around. He can see you safely home."

"No. No, I want to go alone. I want to be alone."

"Elsa, it's not safe for you to be alone right now. Just let Rick escort you home. I would feel much better knowing someone was with you."

"I don't want anyone with me. Please, just let me go alone."

Uncle Clancy stared at her for a moment. His eyes twitched and narrowed as though he wanted to tell her no and tell her that she had to take Rick or else not go anywhere. Thoughts of how to escape the theater should he not let her leave began rolling through her mind, and as she played out each scenario, the more her blood ran cold.

"All right. You can go. I will come to check on you as soon as I finish my work here and finish talking to the sheriff."

"Thank you, Uncle." Her words left a bitter taste on her tongue. Of course, she didn't know if he was involved; she also knew that Rick didn't do anything without her uncle knowing about it. She was even sure Rick told her uncle when he brushed his teeth and combed his hair.

She darted past them, holding her breath as her heart pounded harder and harder until she made her way outside and flagged a carriage passing by. The driver opened the door, and she climbed inside.

"Where are you headed, Miss?" the driver asked.

"Can you take me to the carriage station?"

"Certainly." He tapped the reins against the horse's back, and the carriage rolled down the street.

TWO

JASPER

Jasper had never given much thought to how he'd die. He could assume that being a stagecoach driver, there was a risk of it every time he went out into the wilderness, but still, he never thought about it. Of course, who would? Who would want to imagine such a thing? Only a fool, that's who.

And Jasper Hemlock was no fool.

At least he didn't think he was.

Others might have a different opinion, but he wasn't about to consider what anyone else thought.

"Morning." Jasper's pa looked up from the stove as Jasper entered the kitchen.

"Morning."

"Are you hungry?"

"Not really."

"Well, you should still try to eat. You got to keep up your strength so you can heal." Pa pointed his spatula at Jasper, wiggling it slightly. "I got a fresh batch of pancakes all ready for some butter and syrup."

Although Jasper's stomach rumbled slightly at the mention

of hot pancakes with butter and smothered in syrup, there was also a tiny part of it that twisted with the notion of food. One side wanted the food while the other didn't, and he fought with himself on whether to grab a plate. Catching the sight of the plate of bacon, however, not only gave him an idea but an easy out from a stomach full of pancakes.

"I'll just take some strips of bacon." He reached over and grabbed a few, biting one in half as he headed to the table and sat in a chair, chewing as he pulled one boot on and then the other.

"Where are you going so early this morning?" Pa asked.

"Just for a ride. I need to clear my head. This sitting at home with nothing to do is about to drive me crazy."

"How long are they keeping you off the schedule?"

"Another month." Jasper rolled his eyes, heaving a sigh as a groan whispered through his lips. He'd never taken any time off since starting for the Milton Stagecoach Company—never had the need—until now, and it was for this reason he now knew why. He hated being at home with nothing to do. It wasn't normal. He was meant to work. He was meant to drive the stagecoach from town to town, delivering passengers and living out on the range.

He was also meant to have the use of both of his arms.

Having one in a sling from being shot just wasn't right.

"What did the doctor say the last time he looked at your shoulder?"

"It's healing. But I still can't use it for a few weeks."

"Do you know how lucky you are?" Pa faced Jasper again, folding his arms across his chest. The spatula was tucked under his arm, and a bit of pancake mix smeared across the back of his sleeve.

"Yes, I do. But that doesn't mean I wish to speak about it." Jasper growled under his breath again. It had only been a few short weeks since the Bennett Bandits had attacked the stagecoach he was driving, shooting him in the arm and robbing the passengers. He had fallen from the driver's box and hit his head on a rock, knocking him out. Of course, it had saved his life as the bandits believed him dead. But still, not only had the bandits robbed the stagecoach, but the passengers, a wealthy man, and his wife had made it known to all they knew not only Jasper's name but the stagecoach company he worked for. Since then, his company had seen a less than stellar reputation.

He didn't need the gossip hanging over his head any more than he already had an injury plaguing him.

"Well, perhaps this has been a blessing from God." Pa turned around and flipped another few pancakes in the cast iron pan, smiling as he mumbled about their perfect brown color. "I do make good pancakes," he whispered.

"A blessing from God?" Jasper ignored the pancake comment and focused on the one he thought was the most ridiculous. "Are you seriously trying to say it was a blessing from God that I was shot in the shoulder, knocked out, my passengers robbed—"

"Every dollar and piece of jewelry that was stolen from them was returned."

"That doesn't make it right. It also doesn't make the situation less horrible or traumatic for them. I heard his wife still has nightmares."

"My point is not that what happened was a blessing, but that because of what happened, you now have some time to reflect on what you want in life."

Jasper rolled his eyes and slapped his hand down on the table. There it was—the real reason for the conversation and the one, his Pa, tried to bring up daily.

"Don't you dare start on that again, old man. You know I don't want to talk about things like that."

"I know you don't want to, but maybe you should. Maybe it's time to think about settling down." Pa slid the spatula under each pancake, laying them on the plate before pouring more batter into the hot pan. The batter sizzled and bubbled. After he'd made a few more pancakes, he lifted the plate to his face, inhaling a deep breath before he set it down in the middle of the table. "I've always loved the smell of pancakes. They reminded me of your mama."

Pancakes had always been Jasper's mama's way of showing love. She made them all the time. Even if it wasn't breakfast time, but was instead supper time. He didn't know how many nights he'd enjoy them before bed instead of stew or chili like the rest of his friends in school. She loved making them, and she loved serving them. To the point where she always made more than needed, feeding them to the chickens after her husband, son, and she had their fill.

"Yeah, they always remind me of her too." Jasper looked at the stack in front of him, and part of him got lost in a sea of memories as though his brain needed a moment of distraction. "But don't think changing the subject is going to help."

Pa held up his hands before grabbing the spatula once more. "I wasn't trying to."

"Well, if you were. I'm just letting you know it won't work."

"And why is that?"

"You know that I'm not thinking about those types of things like love and marriage. It's just not for me."

Pa flipped the pancakes in the pan, smiling again at them before turning back to Jasper. "And why is that again?"

"Don't play dumb. You know why. For one, I don't have the time, and for two, I don't know how many other stagecoach drivers have always told me not to get involved with a woman or have children. It's just too risky in our line of work. I don't want to leave a widow or orphans behind."

"Still, though, I would think . . . don't you even want to think about it? I mean, don't you want to know what it's like?"

Jasper opened his mouth but stopped himself before he uttered a word. He didn't know what he wanted to say, or more importantly, didn't know what he wanted to admit. Only a fool wouldn't think about loving a woman or having children of his own. Sure, he thought of it. Each time he'd see a pretty lady walking through town, thoughts would cross his mind. But still, even with those thoughts, he knew what he would leave behind if something happened. Him sitting at the table with one arm in a sling while he recovered from a gunshot was proof of that, and he didn't want to do that to a woman.

But to admit all of this to his pa?

He knew if he did, the old man would never let him hear the end of it. He would bug him day in and day out, asking about it. Not that he didn't already do that, but if he knew the truth, it would make it so much worse.

So, he decided to lie. "No, I don't. It's just not fair to anyone. Besides, I see how lonely you are now that Mama is gone. Even if I lived until a ripe old age, like you, I'd still feel a loss of something I don't ever want to feel."

"Oh, that's nothing more than just another excuse. And a bad one at that." Pa moved toward the table, grabbing the plate of pancakes so he could stack the newly done ones on top of the other ones.

"It's not bad. Not if it makes sense. Which is does."

Pa turned off the stove, setting down the spatula before sitting at the table and serving himself a few pancakes. "You're living your life based on things that haven't—and might not—happened. What kind of a life is that?" He paused for a moment, but before Jasper could say anything, he continued, not even glancing up from spreading a thick layer of butter on the pancakes on his plate. "No need to answer my question because there isn't one. Bottom line, it's not a life. At least not a good one. God never meant for us to live in so much fear that we don't live at all."

"I know that. And I'm not living in fear. I'm choosing to protect someone. How can that be a terrible thing?"

"Because you aren't protecting anyone. You're just making excuses."

"Well, I don't think I am."

Pa grabbed the pitcher of syrup, pouring it over the stack of pancakes. He let out a deep sigh, shaking his head. "I think you are. You just don't want to admit it."

Although Jasper had a lot of fight left in him, he stopped himself from saying anything else. It wasn't worth it. Besides, he doubted there was anything he could say to change Pa's mind.

"I'm going for a ride. I'll be back later."

"Are you sure you don't want to eat anything before you go?"

Jasper glanced over his shoulder at the pancakes on the table. His stomach growled again, but it also twisted with the thought of eating.

"Nah. Just give them to the chickens. They will enjoy them more than I will this morning." Without another word, he left the kitchen, stepping outside into the early morning air.

THREE

ELSA

The stagecoach bounced and rolled down the lane, and with each bump of a rock or dip in the road, her rump ached a little more. She was tired of the stagecoach and tired of riding inside. She didn't know how much further she would be traveling, but she knew that she would have a tough time convincing herself to ride in a stagecoach ever again once she got there.

Of course, her emotional state didn't help either. She had so many questions as to why Rick would attack her that she had stopped asking them. It was pointless as she would never have the answers. She wanted to believe Uncle Clancy wasn't involved either, but at the same time, she couldn't be sure he wasn't. With Rick so stuck in Uncle Clancy's back pocket, those two were as thick as thieves; she once heard someone say when describing them.

Why would they want her hurt? Or worse, why would they want her dead.

"Are you traveling to Lone Hollow, too?" a woman's voice asked.

Elsa glanced up, meeting the gaze of the other passenger. The older woman traveled with an even older man and another younger woman who had spent the whole trip huddled in a corner, not uttering a single word and not even looking up from her hands in her lap.

Surely, her neck ached, Elsa thought to herself.

"I don't have a destination in mind. I was planning on stopping whenever."

The woman and man both blinked at her, and the woman's mouth gaped open. "Oh. Well, isn't that an interesting twist to one's travels?"

Although the woman tried to hide her true thoughts, her tone spoke of how she wanted to turn up her nose to Elsa's decision. At least, that was the impression she gave. A young woman traveling alone was one thing, but a young lady traveling alone without a destination in mind, just riding the waves of her imagination, that was another.

For a moment, Elsa thought to elaborate on her answer, or perhaps correct herself in telling the woman, she did plan on stopping in the town she mentioned, but something stopped her. She didn't care what the woman's opinion of her was.

She glanced out of the window of the stagecoach, ignoring how she could feel the woman's eyes still burning into the side of her face. She had too much else to worry about in life right now to give any attention to a snob.

"Sorry to bother you again," the woman said. "But you look familiar to me. Do we know each other?"

Elsa looked back at her, trying to give her best fake smile. She'd learned it a while ago when dealing with the public and fans when she didn't want to. "I'm sorry, but I don't think so."

"I just feel like I've seen you someplace before." The woman giggled and fidgeted with her hands. "Oh, don't mind me. I don't have much for memory at my age. For all I know, you could look like someone I know."

While a small part of Elsa wanted to ask the woman if she'd ever been to the Millwood Theater in Butte, she also didn't know if she wanted the couple to know who she was. Wasn't she fleeing Butte to get away from anyone and everyone who might recognize her or know her?

"Perhaps that's it," she said instead. "I've been told I have a familiar face, but for the most part, it's from people whom I don't know."

The wagon lurched, and Elsa grabbed onto the window frame.

"What on earth was that?" the woman asked her husband.

As they glanced at each other, the wagon gave another lurch.

However, before anyone could say anything this time, the horses seemed to take off, and the wagon sped down the road. Each time it hit a dip in the road or a rock, the force and the speed would cause the stagecoach to teeter from one side to the other. Both the older woman and the younger one screamed. The man wrapped his arm around his wife's shoulder, and he mumbled a few words. His voice grew louder and louder every time the wagon teetered.

"It's going to be all right, Madeline. It's going to be all right."

Elsa stuck her body half out of the window, but the wind ripped through her hair, slapping it against her face and blocking her sight. No matter how many times she moved the strands, they would whip around more, and she finally sat back on the inside of the carriage again.

The stagecoach picked up more speed, barreling down the road. It turned slightly, and Elsa felt the side lift. She imagined the wheels coming off the ground but spinning just the same from the speed. She held her breath and closed her eyes, waiting for the wheels to touch back down.

A prayer whispered across her lips, and although she had hoped they would be all right, as the stagecoach seemed to continue to tip over more and more, she realized they might be in more trouble than she thought possible.

The two other women screamed again just as the stagecoach hit another rock. The bounce knocked it off what little balance it had left, and it flipped over, rolling several times. Elsa's head bashed into the window frame and then the top of the stagecoach as her body bounced around along with everyone else . . .

~

She opened her eyes to the dust still settling around her. Her head pounded, and thick, red blood dripped down the side of her cheek. She coughed. Her whole body hurt, and the pain made her cry out. She rolled over on her side, opening her eyes again. Her gaze landed on the stagecoach lying on its side. Broken into pieces in most places, the wheels still spun as though the inertia propelled them to do so.

Where am I, she thought to herself.

She took another few deep breaths, and as she exhaled, dust puffed around her lips, making her cough again. She rolled over onto her stomach, pressing her hands into the dirt as she pushed off the ground. More pain spread through her body, and she heaved herself up onto her knees.

Soreness hitched through her every movement, and as she staggered to her feet, she turned toward the stagecoach. The driver was gone, and three bodies lay around the crash.

She opened her mouth but stopped herself. She didn't know their names.

She stumbled closer to them but catching sight of the blood and their mangled bodies, she stopped and turned away.

Her breath quickened, and the world around her spun. Stars speckled across her vision, and her knees buckled. She hit the ground.

~

JASPER

Jasper wanted nothing more than a relaxing ride where he could not think about anything other than the nature around him. He wanted to immerse himself in the trees and tall grass, listening to the birds chirping in the sunlight.

Instead, he could think of nothing else but the conversation with Pa.

He didn't want to replay it in his mind, and yet that was all he did, and each time he thought the words marriage, wife, and children, he snorted.

Even if he wanted those things—which he didn't—it was a terrible idea. He knew it. He just wished his pa knew it too.

He glanced up at the sky, then down at the ground, blowing out a breath. His eyes traced along the rocks around the road, but as he took them all in, he also noticed deep grooves in the road. As though a wagon came through the area at a varying amount of speed. He glanced around, narrowing his gaze as the tracks continued up ahead. Not only were rocks displaced, but bushes had been trampled, pushed aside by speeding horses and a stagecoach.

He halted his horse.

Concern began to bubble in his chest. Something wasn't right. Something happened.

He cued the horse forward, following the path through the damaged brush at a trot. Although his shoulder hurt, he continued until he reached a cliff. He stopped again as he saw the skid marks in the dirt, and he swung his leg over, dismounting the horse. He rushed to the edge of the cliff, both wanting to know what happened and not wanting to see the scene he could imagine in his mind.

Closing his eyes for a moment, he took a deep breath and gazed down at the bottom of the ravine. A stagecoach sat on its side. Broken in so many places, it was one of the worst crashes he'd ever seen. He counted three, no four bodies, and he rushed down the side of the hill toward them. While he didn't know if he'd find any survivors, he hoped he would.

He knelt by a young woman, checking her pulse. Nothing.

Then he moved on to an older woman and a man, lying near one another. Both of them were deceased too. The last woman lay in the dirt not far from the stagecoach, and as he bent down and pressed his fingers into the side of her neck, she moved and made a soft grunting noise.

"Ma'am? Ma'am, can you hear me? Ma'am, are you hurt anywhere?" He shook his head at how foolish the question sounded, but it was the only thing he could think to ask. "Ma'am, can you hear me?"

She moved a little more, and her eyes fluttered open.

"Ma'am, can you hear me?"

She blinked at him and nodded.

"Are you too hurt to move?"

She shook her head.

"All right. Just . . ." He glanced around him, trying to think of what to do. Water. Get her water. "Wait here one moment. Don't move, all right?"

She nodded again.'

He stood up and rushed over to the stagecoach, looking through the inside of the carriage and around the driver's box for a canteen. After finding one, he twisted the cap, opening it as he made his way back to the woman.

He knelt beside her again. "I'm going to lift your head, all right?"

She nodded.

His knees dug in the dirt as he slid his arm under her neck and lifted it until it could rest on his knee. With her head lifted, he brought the canteen to her lips, tilting it until the water spilled out and into her mouth. She took several sips then he laid her head back down.

"Do you think you can stand up?" he asked.

She hesitated for a second, then nodded and moved as though trying to sit up. He wrapped his arm around her, helping her.

"Do you know what happened?"

She shook her head and opened her mouth. Her voice failed her, cracking on her words until she dropped it to a whisper. "No, I don't. We were traveling along the road when suddenly the stagecoach just started speeding along. It was like the driver lost control. The next thing I know, we started turning and then rolling."

"The horses must have broken free around the turn." He glanced up toward the top of the ravine. "I didn't see where the driver went. But the stagecoach must have rolled down the hill. We should get you to the doctor in town. It's not far." He paused, taking in the sight of the crash as he heaved a deep breath. "I'm sorry to tell you that your family didn't survive."

"Family?" she whispered.

He motioned toward the bodies lying near the stagecoach. "Your family."

She shook her head. "They aren't my family. At least . . . at least I don't think they are. I don't think I know who they are. I mean, I don't feel like I know who they are."

"You don't feel like you know them?" He cocked his head, raising one eyebrow.

"No, I don't." She shook her head. Tears pooled in her eyes, and she wiped them away before they streamed down her cheeks.

"It's all right. You don't need to cry. We will figure out who they are in another way. What is your name, miss?"

She opened her mouth but stopped before she said a word. Her eyes widened, and she sucked in a breath.

"What's the matter?" he asked.

"I . . . I don't know my name. I don't know who I am."

FOUR

JASPER

After stopping by the Sheriff's Office and sharing the news of the crash with Sheriff Bullock and Deputy Sheriff Harrison, Jasper took the young woman to the doctor. She rode on the horse in front of him in silence, and her body trembled against his. He didn't want to think about what she was going through, nor did he want to think about how confusing everything must be right now for her. She didn't know who she was, where she was, or why she was even on the stagecoach.

"I'll take you to the doctor now," he said, keeping his voice light. "And I apologize if you're uncomfortable."

She shook her head. "You don't have to apologize. I'm not uncomfortable."

She adjusted her weight and ducked her chin as they continued to the doctor, and after they arrived at the house in the middle of town, he climbed off, tying the reins around the tie post before making his way back around to the side of the horse.

"Do you need help down?"

"No. I think I can manage."

He watched as she swung her leg over. Her arms and legs twitched, and she struggled as her feet hit the ground. Her knees buckled, and he lunged forward, wrapping his good arm around her before she hit the ground. While he expected her to fight against his grip—he was a stranger after all—she didn't. Instead, she clutched onto his shirt, grabbing his sleeves so tight he worried her nails would rip the seams.

"It's all right," he said. "I've got you. I won't let you fall." He held her tighter until she regained her balance and eased up to stand. "Are you all right?"

"Yes." She tucked her chin and her face flushed with a slight pink color. "Thank you. I'm sorry to be such a bother."

"You aren't. Let's get you inside, though, before it happens again." He kept his hand on the small of her back as he led her up the pathway and across the porch to the door. He knocked, waiting until another man answered it.

"Mr. Hemlock? What brings you here today?" The man glanced from Jasper to the woman, and his mouth gaped open. He didn't utter another word.

"Good afternoon, Dr. Miller. I came across this young woman on the road. She was in a stagecoach accident."

Dr. Miller's eyes widened. "Oh, well, come in. Come in." He opened the door wider, motioning the two to come inside. "Let's get you in the office." He led them down a hallway into another room lined with beds. Jasper had already seen enough of this room for his liking, and the sight of it only made a nervous itch crawl up his skin. He'd spent a few days in this very room after the doctor dug the bullet out of his shoulder, telling Pa he would regain the use of his arm, but it would take a while.

"Have a seat," the doctor said to the woman. She followed his order and sat down. Her eyes were misted with tears, and the doctor paused. "Where are you hurt?" he asked.

She shook her head. "I'm not. At least I don't think I am."

"Well, it does say a lot that you walked in here this afternoon. I don't see any broken bones from how you are moving." He nodded toward his hands, then looked at her neck and jawline. "May I?"

"Yes."

With her permission, he clutched the sides of her face, checking her eyes and ears before he twisted her head from side to side.

"Any pain?"

She shook her head. "Just soreness."

"The rest of the people perished in the accident. She doesn't know if they are her family." Jasper shoved his hands in his pants pockets and shrugged.

Dr. Miller blinked at him, then turned toward the woman. "How do you not know if they are your family?"

"She doesn't know who she is," Jasper answered for her.

"Is that true?" the doctor asked her.

She nodded.

"You don't know who you are? You don't know your name?"

She shook her head. More tears welled in her eyes, and as she spoke, even at a whisper, her voice cracked. "I don't know anything."

Dr. Miller straightened his shoulders and heaved a deep sigh. He glanced from Jasper to the woman, then back to Jasper, then turned away from them. He lifted his hand, rubbing his chin and the side of his face as though he was lost in his thoughts and needed something to do.

"Dr. Miller? Can you help her?" Jasper asked.

The doctor spun to face him. "I'm afraid I can't. Memory loss is in the brain, which is a complicated matter in and of itself. Wounds can be treated, stitched, and healed with ointment. But the brain. I can't do anything for her."

"So, she's just supposed to live her life not knowing who she is?"

The woman buried her face in her hands with his question, and guilt pricked through his skin. He hadn't meant to be so insensitive or to make her cry.

"Are you sure there isn't anything you can do, Dr. Miller?"

"All I know of brain injuries is that they are unpredictable. Sometimes with time, the patients regain their full memories. Other times they get only a little or most of them but not all. It's hard to say what her outcome will be. She needs time."

"And what is she supposed to do in the meantime?"

"Along with time, she needs a place of comfort. A place she can feel safe. If she feels secure, her brain will have a better chance of healing."

"I understand that. But where is that place? It's not like I can take her home. I don't know who she is."

The two men stared at one another before they glanced back toward the woman. She still had her face buried in her hands, and another sting of guilt prickled in Jasper's chest. He had been talking about her as though she wasn't in the room. And talking rather loudly, he might add. She didn't need him shouting her problem from the rooftops as though she didn't know what was going on or the trials she was facing. She needed compassion. She needed kindness.

"Ma'am, I'm . . . I'm sorry," he said.

She looked away from her hands. Her eyes were red and swollen, and tears streamed down her cheeks.

The sight of her only made him feel worse about how he acted.

"What if I put her up in a room at the hotel. I don't mind even if it takes a few weeks."

"Weeks?" Dr. Miller cocked his head to the side, and Jasper didn't like the way he narrowed his eyes, and a crease formed on his forehead. "Of course, there is a chance it could take just weeks; there is also the chance it could take a lot longer than that for her brain to heal and her memories to return. Plus, a hotel room. Alone. That won't be where she will find the comfort and safety she will need."

"So, what are you suggesting?"

"She needs a home environment with people around her to help her feel a sense of security."

Jasper moved toward the doctor and lowered his voice. "And just what am I supposed to do with that? Shall I go door-to-door in the town of Lone Hollow, asking every family if they will take a strange woman in for who knows how long?"

"Well, why can't she stay in your guesthouse?"

Jasper sucked in a breath, nearly choking on a bit of spit that went down the wrong pipe. He coughed and sputtered for several minutes, holding his arm toward the doctor and nodding after he asked if Jasper was all right. His eyes burned and filled with tears that he wiped away.

"I'm sorry, but what did you say?"

"Why can't she stay in your guesthouse? It's not like you are leaving for work on the stagecoach any time soon, and if you heal and leave, your pa is there to see to her needs."

"We can't take care of her."

"Why not?"

"We are two men? Who know nothing about . . . nothing."

"Oh, I don't think that's a problem, and I'm sure your pa would love the company."

"You don't understand."

"Then make me understand because it looks like a fine idea where I'm sitting."

"Well, it isn't a fine idea at all!" Jasper didn't know why he raised his voice to a shout, but after he did, the two men, once again, just stared at one another. "And I think she would agree with me."

The woman turned to both of them. "But I don't," she said. Although her voice was light, it was just enough of a shock to make Jasper flinch.

~

ELSA

She looked at the two men, blinking at them while they stared at her.

Mr. Hemlock's mouth gaped for a moment, and then he closed it. "Are you saying you agree with the doctor? You want to come to my home?"

"Honestly, I like the thought of a guesthouse, which is more like a home than a hotel room."

"But you don't know me."

"I know you enough to know you are a kind man who has helped a woman after a horrible accident. If you had intentions of hurting me, you would have already done it. And you haven't." She paused for a moment, taking in a long, deep breath. "Not to mention, the doctor knows you. Should anything happen to me, he would know . . ." She let her voice trail off. Not sure she wanted to finish the sentence, she hoped that the words she had uttered gave them enough idea of where she was going with her point.

It was true. He was a stranger. A person she didn't know anything about other than his name. At this point, however, she knew more about him than she knew of herself, and if he had wanted to do her harm, he would have done it already.

"I don't have the time for all of this." Mr. Hemlock spun in a circle, lifting his arm while the one in the sling remained at his side and letting the lifted one slap down against his hip.

The doctor looked over at him, motioning toward the arm in the sling. "Seems you have all the time in the world right now. Besides, she might help you and your pa at the ranch."

Mr. Hemlock spun around again. "Well, I just think this is a crazy idea."

"Crazy to you or not, it makes sense to me. And as long as Miss . . ." The doctor stared at her for a moment. "Miss . . . Smith—"

"Smith?"

"Well, you have to call her something. Miss Smith seems like something common. What do you think, ma'am?"

"Miss Smith is fine."

The doctor turned his attention back to Mr. Hemlock. "As long as Miss Smith is all right with the idea, then it's her wishes we should abide by. It's important for her healing and recovery to be someplace she is comfortable. It will help her, and you never know; it might only be a little while before she regains her memories."

Mr. Hemlock looked at the doctor, then at her, and back at the doctor. He inhaled a deep breath, letting the air puff up his cheeks before exhaling it. "All right. She can stay in my guesthouse."

FIVE

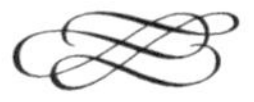

ELSA

Although she had ridden into town on Mr. Hemlock's horse in front of him, he had borrowed a wagon and a horse from a friend in town, Pastor Duncan who seemed like a welcoming, pleasant man. She hadn't minded the saddle as she had far too much else going on in her mind to think about the strange man sitting right behind her or the fact that his body was pressed against hers. But now, she was grateful for the wagon and the space it gave them both.

"So, Miss . . . Smith . . . do you remember anything? Like, do you know what that is called?" He pointed to the horse.

"Yes, I know. It's a horse. And this is a wagon, and we are sitting on a seat. I do know those things."

"Well, I guess that's a start. The others in the stagecoach, can you remember anything about them?"

"No."

"Well, perhaps, Sheriff Bullock can find out who they are." He slapped the reins on the back of the horse, and the horse obliged the command for more speed. He picked up a trot and continued down the lane through the trees.

"How far do you live outside of town?" she asked, glancing

all around her as the sunlight flecked down upon them through the branches.

"Not far. Just a few miles. It's my pa's ranch, not mine. I live there with him when I'm not running on the stagecoach."

"What do you mean?"

"I'm a stagecoach driver."

"Oh." Her heart thumped at the word stagecoach, and she glanced down at her hands, fidgeting with them as she tried to remember what happened in the accident. The last she remembered was waking up to Mr. Hemlock talking to her, and she had no recollection of how she'd gotten there or what had happened.

"But I'm not doing any runs for a while." He let out a chuckle as he nodded toward the sling in his arm.

"What happened? If you don't mind my asking."

"I was shot by some bandits trying to hold up the stagecoach so they could rob my passengers."

"That's awful. Did your passengers . . . are they all right?"

"They were traumatized, but they were unharmed. The sheriff managed to apprehend one of them, and he shot the others before they could kill his wife."

"They were going to kill his wife?" Miss Smith gaped at him. This story was getting worse by the second. "What kind of a town is Lone Hollow?"

He chuckled again. "Oh, this wasn't exactly in Lone Hollow, and it's a rather long story. But don't worry. It's a safe town. Sometimes terrible things just happened. Even to good people."

"I suppose I understand that."

They continued down the lane in silence, and although she glanced at him a few times, neither one of them said a word. While she didn't know his reasons, she knew hers. It wasn't that she didn't have questions she wanted to ask or things she wanted to say; it was that she didn't know if she could physically bring herself to ask or say them.

"There's the ranch," he said, pointing toward a cabin that emerged through the trees. Another smaller cabin rested several hundred feet from the larger one, and there was another building, the biggest of all three, and it stood a little off to the side. Dozens of chickens roamed around it, pecking and scratching the ground as they feasted on the bugs they could find. "I'll get my pa, and he can get you settled in while I return the horse and wagon to Pastor Duncan."

"Oh. All right."

"I was going to get some supplies at the general store for you too. Food for you to eat and . . . do you need anything else?"

"No, I don't think so. Just food would be fine."

"I'm assuming you know how to cook."

She opened her mouth but paused and hesitated. She knew what food was and could remember different cuts of meat and the different types of fruit and vegetables. She knew what bread was and cakes and pies. Perhaps if she was in a kitchen surrounded by ingredients, she could prepare a meal.

"I think so," she said.

"Well, I'll get you some things, and I'll also stop by the sheriff's office to collect the bags he told me he would collect from the accident. Maybe going through them will bring something back to you." He pulled the wagon to a halt in front of the main house, and as he climbed down from the wagon and moved around it to help her down, the front door of the house opened. An older man stepped out with a pipe in his hand. He stared at them for a moment, then cocked one eyebrow as he slowly made his way from the porch down to the wagon.

"I didn't mean for you to go out and get married today. I thought you were going for a ride."

Mr. Hemlock glanced over his shoulder at the man and groaned. "Would you hush about that? I did go out for a ride. I came across a stagecoach accident and . . . well, this woman was a survivor."

"And you thought to bring her here. Why exactly?" The older man took a couple of puffs on his pipe, and the smoke billowed around his head.

Mr. Hemlock turned to face his father. "She got injured and doesn't know who she is."

"And you told her she was your wife?" The older man gave his son a wink and laughed, and although the moment was more odd than funny, the way he mocked his son made her laugh a little, too.

"No, you old fart!" Mr. Hemlock rubbed his forehead then ran his hands through his hair. A hint of amusement echoed in his tone along with annoyance. "The doctor thought if she was in a comfortable place that she might get her memories back sooner. He thought she could keep you company and help out around here."

"Well, he wasn't exactly wrong, was he?" The older man leaned over, looking around his son. "Good evening, ma'am."

She nodded. "Good evening."

"So, she doesn't know her name?" The older man asked his son.

Mr. Hemlock shook his head. "The doctor gave her the name Miss Smith."

The older man made a face, crinkling one side of his lips and nose. "Well, that won't do. She needs a pretty name, one that fits that beautiful face." He rubbed his chin with his fingers, then pointed at her. "What about Emma?"

Mr. Hemlock cocked his head to the side. "Do you think that is a good idea?"

"Why not? The only other Emma I knew was the most beautiful woman in the world. I think it fits." The older man moved toward the wagon as she climbed down, and he stuck his hand out as he neared her. "It's nice to meet you, Miss Emma Smith. You like the name, don't you?"

"Yes, I do. It's a beautiful name."

"My name is Benjamin Hemlock, and I want to welcome you to my home."

"Thank you."

"I thought you could get her settled in the guest house while I return the wagon and horse to Pastor Duncan." Young Mr. Hemlock made his way back to the wagon, climbing up into the seat. "Do you think you can manage that?"

"Of course, I can. I'm not an incapable fool." Old Mr. Hemlock waved his hands at his son. "We'll be just fine without you. Don't you worry."

"Oh, I'm more than worried." The two men chuckled at each other, and then young Mr. Hemlock pointed to his father. "Don't be filling this lady's head with all your nonsense either."

Old Mr. Hemlock waved his hand again. "Just go. You don't want to be riding back in the dark. We'll be fine." He glanced at Emma, winking at her. "Won't we?"

She couldn't help but smile at his mirth, and she nodded. "Yes, we will."

They waved their last goodbye as the young Mr. Hemlock cued the horse back out onto the lane and settled into a brisk pace back toward town. Emma watched him until he vanished in the trees, then she turned to old Mr. Hemlock.

"Are you ready to see the guest house?" he asked.

She nodded.

He motioned her to follow him, and as he shuffled along, his boots left long marks in the dirt. "So, you really can't remember anything, huh?"

"No, Sir. I can't."

"Oh, there's no need for the 'sir.' And don't worry about calling me Mr. Hemlock, either. You're more than welcome to call me Benjamin."

"All right. Since you gave me the name, I guess you're more than welcome to call me Emma."

He glanced over his shoulder and winked at her. "I was already planning on it."

"Is there a reason you picked that name?" she asked as she quickened her pace and moved up alongside him instead of behind him.

"It was my wife's name. She was a beautiful woman, inside and out. She was always one to help anyone in need. Just a wonderful soul."

"What happened to her?"

"Well, that's the thing, we don't know. We found her near the barn, and she was just gone. No one knows what happened."

"I'm so sorry for your loss."

"Thank you." He tucked his chin and sniffed, then looked up. "She would have thought you were just beautiful, however. And she would have felt so bad that you lost all your memories." As they reached the porch of the guest house, he stopped and faced her. "You don't have any memories at all?"

"No. I've been trying to think of something . . . anything . . . but I can't. Mr. Hemlock is hopeful that when he brings the luggage retrieved from the accident, it might spur something."

"Well, hopefully, it does."

He continued across the porch and opened the door to the guest house. She followed him, stepping into the older cabin before spinning around to take the sight of it all in.

Although older and layered with a thick coat of dust, it was comfortable, homey, like a warm blanket she could wrap around her shoulders on a cold night and feel a sense of relief, even if it was just a bit.

"It's lovely," she said.

"It's dirty." Benjamin chuckled as he shut the door, made his way over to the windows in the front, and opened the curtains. The movement shook even more dust free, and the particles floated in the air, visible from the rays of the sunset shining in the window. "I can help you clean it if you like."

"Oh, no, that won't be necessary. It will give me something to do. Perhaps it will help."

Benjamin studied her for a moment, closing one eye as he looked at her from her shoes up to her head. "I think I'll bring you my wife's old trunk. It's full of dresses and work clothes, and I think you two might be around about the same size. Just until Jasper gets back with the luggage."

"That would be nice."

"Well, then I'll fetch it for you and then leave you to settle in. I want to invite you for dinner tonight. Over at the main house. If you would like."

"Dinner would be nice, too."

"Great." He hooked his thumb over his shoulder. "I shall be right back."

She watched Benjamin leave, shutting the door behind him. Finally, alone in the cabin, she made her way over to the small bed and sat down, heaving a deep sigh as her rump hit the layer of blankets. Another bit of dust puffed around her; some of it settled back down on the bed while the rest made its way to the floor. She heaved a couple of deep breaths and glanced around at the room. Her eyes traced over the table and chairs sitting near the kitchen, the stove in the corner, the curtains hanging from all the windows, and lastly, the different shelves on the walls. Each one held either oil lanterns or books. It had nothing fancy, but it was warm and comfortable, even with all the dust and the cobwebs in the corner—all of which just needed a good cleaning and a brush with a broom.

I might as well get to work, she thought.

She heaved herself off the bed, moving over to the kitchen and opening each of the cabinets, searching for a rag, broom, and dustpan. She looked for memories in each movement, but nothing so far had triggered anything.

SIX

ELSA (EMMA)

Emma stared down at the luggage lying on the bed in front of her. The first had been full of men's clothes, and she had already discarded it to the floor, buckling it tight before propping it up so Mr. Hemlock could take it back to the sheriff.

The other three bags were full of women's clothes, and while one of them had garments that looked a little too big for her, the other two were similar in size. The only difference between them was the style. One had more plain type dresses while the other had dresses made with more lace and frills with brighter colors. Looking down upon the dress she was wearing, her guess was the latter of the bags was hers.

The one with more lace and frills.

And the choice of dresses only made her wonder about who she was even more. Did she come from a wealthy family? Or was she just someone who liked the finer things in life, dressing in bright colors to stand out in a crowd?

While there was a tiny part of her still drawn to the dresses, the way she felt at this moment, she also set aside the bag she believed was hers and donned the plainer and more mundane apparel, even if it was perhaps the clothes of a stranger.

A knock rapped on the door, and she made her way over to it, opening it.

"Good evening, Miss Smith," Mr. Hemlock said, tipping his hat. "I hope I'm not bothering you."

"No, not at all."

"Did the luggage help?" He lifted his eyebrows, and a crease moved through his forehead, exaggerating the hopeful tone in his voice.

She didn't want to say no and disappoint him, but she didn't want to lie either. "No. I'm sorry they didn't."

"Oh, well, that's nothing to apologize for. Maybe they still can. Maybe the doctor was right, and all you need is time."

"Maybe."

"My pa said he invited you to dinner, and I was just making sure you didn't need anything before I start preparing supper."

"No, I don't. But . . . I'd like to help."

"You would?"

"Of course. You two have done so much for me, and it's only right that I help around here. Besides, I think it would be good for me to do something that distracts me from my thoughts."

"You're more than welcome to help. I was about to go out to the chicken coop to get the chicken for tonight. Do you want to come?"

"Let me just grab a wrap that I found in one of the bags."

After securing the wrap around her shoulders, Emma followed Mr. Hemlock to the barn. The sun had begun to set, and colors of pink and purple splashed across the sky, illuminating the white, puffy clouds.

"It's a beautiful night," she said, drawing the wrap tighter around her.

"I was thinking that very thing on my ride back home. Oh, I

have the supplies for you in the house. After supper, I'll take them over to the guest house. It's not much, but it will last you about a week. I didn't know if you wanted to commit to all your meals with us." He chuckled under his breath as he opened the door to the chicken coop.

The chickens scattered throughout the coop, squawking and flapping their wings as they fled. Mr. Hemlock rushed toward several who had taken refuge in the corner of the coop, and he grabbed one by its legs, holding it upside down while it squawked and tried to fly.

Emma closed her eyes, cringing at the thought of the chicken's fate. Although she knew where food came from, the idea of it still made her uneasy.

"You don't have to watch if you don't want," Mr. Hemlock said, noticing her movement.

She smiled and nodded, and as he passed her, carrying the struggling chicken, the feeling that she'd lived through this moment hit her in the chest. She sucked in a breath, picturing the moment in her mind. She was a little girl, perhaps no more than ten or eleven years old, and she was standing in the chicken coop while her father walked toward her. Although she couldn't see his face in her head, she felt as though it was someone she cared about.

"Miss Smith?" Mr. Hemlock stopped and cocked his head to the side. "Are you all right?"

"I remembered something. My father was getting one of our chickens for supper. I lived on a ranch when I was a girl. We had chickens."

"Well, that's good."

"It's not clear memory, and it's not one I can use."

"But it's still something. Your mind is trying. I think it's a good thing." He paused for a moment, glancing between her and the house. "Why don't you go in and help my pa. It's probably better for you to be inside than outside right now, and while I don't think I need the help, I know he will. He likes to think he's a great cook and while I'd agree with him on that with a few things, making fried potatoes isn't one of his strengths." Mr. Hemlock chuckled at his joke and winked at her.

She smiled. "Are you sure you don't need help?"

"Nah. I'll get this hen taken care of and will be in shortly after I pluck it."

She left Mr. Hemlock, making her way toward the house while he continued around to the side of the barn. She tried to remember the pictured image of her father, focusing on the man's face as he walked past her. No matter how many times she tried to think of what he looked like, he remained nothing more than a blur, and she growled to herself as she knocked on the door and waited for Benjamin to open it.

"Let me guess," he said after greeting her. "He told you I can't make fried potatoes."

"Something like that."

Benjamin motioned for her to come inside, and after she walked through the doorframe, he leaned out, cupping his hand to the side of his mouth before he shouted. "I make fried potatoes better than him!"

Before Mr. Hemlock could shout back a retort, Benjamin slammed the door and smiled at Emma.

"If I'm being honest, I don't make them better. He was right to send you in here."

"Well, I'm not sure I can do any better than what you do." She laughed and threw her hands up in the air.

"I guess we will find out." Benjamin motioned toward the kitchen, following after her as she made her way over to the stove.

She glanced down at the cut-up potatoes in the skillet. Large chunks of lard were dolloped throughout the starchy vegetables, and as Benjamin opened the stove, tossing in more pieces of wood to heat it, the lard began to melt, and the potatoes started to sizzle.

"I always add some onion to it, but Jasper doesn't like onions. Do you like onions, Emma?" Benjamin asked.

She nodded.

"Well, at least you remember that." Benjamin grabbed a white onion lying on the side of a cutting board and hacked it open with a large knife. The rude smell hit her nose, and her eyes burned until she moved away from it.

"It's odd," she said. "I remember some things and yet not others. I don't understand it."

"Has anything triggered your memories?"

"Yes. The chickens outside. I grew up on a farm, or at least we had chickens." She reached over near where Benjamin was still cutting up the onion, grabbing a bowl full of salt. She pinched some, sprinkling it on the potatoes as they cooked, and as Benjamin finished with the onions and dumped them into the skillet, she gave the mixture another light dusting of the white seasoning.

They continued to cook, mainly chatting about the guest-house and how she liked it. There was a comforting way about Benjamin, and she found herself enjoying their time just as much as preparing the meal.

It wasn't long before Jasper came inside, carrying the plucked and gutted chicken, and with a layer of even more salt and pepper, he plopped it into a pan and stuck it in the oven.

"Now, all we have to do is wait," he said.

~

After finishing the last bites on their plates, both Benjamin and Mr. Hemlock leaned back in their chairs and patted their stomachs. It was like watching a mirrored image of one man, and their movement made Emma smile.

Whether they knew how much they were alike or not, it was amusing to watch.

"I think those might just be the best fried potatoes you have made, Pa," Mr. Hemlock said. He lifted his finger, stopping his father from speaking. "Although I guess that's because you didn't make them."

"Oh, hush. I did too. Or at least I helped."

"All you did was cut up the potatoes and onions, which I still don't like, but since the potatoes were good, I didn't mind." He pointed toward the pile of cooked onions he'd picked out of his supper still sitting in one corner of his plate. "At least tell me you watched Miss Smith, so you learned how she made them."

"Yeah, I watched her. Didn't see anything that I don't do, though." The older man continued to mumble under his breath, grumbling words Emma couldn't hear for a moment before he glanced up at her. "What did you think, Emma? Did you like it?"

"Yes. Everything was delicious. Thank you for inviting me to join you tonight."

"Of course. I wouldn't have it any other way. In fact, you're invited to breakfast tomorrow morning. I can make you my famous pancakes."

"Famous, huh?" Mr. Hemlock said, cocking his head to the side.

"Don't you start with me, boy. You know all too well I make the best pancakes this side of the Montana border."

Mr. Hemlock laughed and looked at Emma. "I'm just playing with him. In all honesty, they are the best pancakes."

"That's right!" Benjamin pointed toward his son, wiggling his finger. "And don't you forget it. I got the recipe from your mama, and she was the best cook I've ever known. Even better than Boots in town, and that's saying a lot."

Mr. Hemlock gave a hissed breath, then chuckled as though his thoughts were funny. "You better not let Boots hear you saying something like that. He might not allow us to eat in the café anymore."

Emma watched the pair glancing between them through their back-and-forth banter. She couldn't help but smile, and an overwhelming sense of comfort washed through her shoulders as she inhaled and exhaled a couple of deep breaths. While it was no surprise the two men seemed to fit with one another, as she would expect most fathers and sons do, these two were more entertaining than she could have imagined. Their wit and banter warmed her soul, and she could see that even though they mocked one another, there was nothing but family love between them.

While she wanted to soak it all in, a tiny part of her felt a little envious, and she hoped that when she finally remembered who she was and where she was from, there was a family like this one waiting for her.

"Aside from breakfast, though, you should probably let Miss Smith have some privacy. I'm sure she doesn't want to eat every meal with us. Besides, I got her enough supplies to last her a few days. As the doctor said, we should let her rest."

"Rest. That's not what she needs. She needs to have conversations and people around her. In fact, I think we should take her to church tomorrow."

"I don't think she wants to—"

"Don't say that until you ask her." Benjamin pointed toward Emma, and before Mr. Hemlock could even turn to look at her, Benjamin asked. "What do you think about it, Emma? Would you like to come to church with us tomorrow?"

"I don't think it's a good idea, so if you want to say no, Miss Smith, we understand." Mr. Hemlock glanced between them before staring at his plate. Her jaw clenched, and his brow furrowed as though he had more to say but didn't know if he should.

Although nervousness fluttered in her stomach at the

thought of meeting a town full of strangers, she couldn't deny it was everything she had hoped for as soon as he mentioned it.

"I would love to," she said.

"Wonderful. Pancakes and God. What more could anyone want?" Benjamin chuckled as he slapped his son on the back of the shoulder.

His optimism was intoxicating.

SEVEN

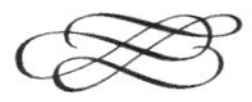

ELSA (EMMA)

"And so it says in *Ecclesiastes 3*, To everything, there is a season, A time for every purpose under heaven: A time to be born, And a time to die, a time to plant, and a time to pluck what is planted; a time to kill, and a time to heal, a time to break down, and a time to build up; a time to weep, and a time to laugh; a time to mourn, and a time to dance; a time to cast away stones, and a time to gather stones; a time to embrace, and a time to refrain from embracing; a time to gain, and a time to lose; a time to keep, and a time to throw away; a time to tear, and a time to sew; a time to keep silence, and a time to speak; a time to love, and a time to hate; a time of war, and a time of peace."

As Pastor Duncan finished the verse, he held up his hands, pointing to different townsfolk in the pews, and continued. "I ask you, do you know what time are you in your life right now? Are you hurting, whether in pain emotionally or physically? Or are you enjoying all that God has given you and are living in a sense of peace? Are you troubled in another way? Perhaps you have questions in your heart and mind, questions that no one can answer? What time is it in your life? Remember as you reflect on this today and pray in the days to come and to seek out the answers to where you are in life. To give any troubles to God and thank Him for all He has given. No one is lost in the eyes of our Lord, even if they feel it in their hearts. Trust Him. Confide in Him. Give Him what you cannot bear. Let us pray."

With the last of the pastor's words, the men and women sitting around Emma all bowed their heads. She did, too, closing her eyes. She didn't know if she had attended church regularly, but she, at this moment, had wanted to believe she did. Nothing had been more moving in her eyes than this morning, and while she didn't know exactly what she would say to God in her prayers, she knew that no matter what happened, she wanted to put her faith and hope in Him.

"You are dismissed. Have a blessed day." As the pastor finished and smiled at everyone sitting in the church, the townsfolk all stood and began filing out of the pews and through the doors to the world outside. Sunlight beamed through the doorframes, brighter than it had through the painted windows of the church, and the new light brightened the room. Benjamin and Mr. Hemlock both stood, but Pastor Duncan approached them before either of them could move out into the aisle. He nodded toward them, then turned his attention to Emma.

"I was hoping to see you this morning, Miss . . . Smith, right?"

"Yes."

"We decided on Miss Emma Smith." A smile beamed across Benjamin's face while Mr. Hemlock closed his eyes and shook his head. A slight grunt whispered in his chest.

"Miss Emma Smith. I like it. It's a lovely name to have until you remember your real one. Which, speaking of, how have you been feeling?"

"I'm all right."

"Have any memories come back to you?"

"Only one. It was of my father walking past me holding a chicken. His face was blurry, however. But I can assume I lived on some farm, or we had chickens."

"Well, I'm sure that God will help and answer your prayers when He feels it is time. We all have our own time, you know." The pastor winked. "And we never know what His plan is."

"I'm learning that." Her cheeks flushed with heat as Pastor Duncan laughed at her admission.

"We all have learned it, and we do in our own time. I hope you are planning to stay for the picnic we have planned. It would be nice to have you see what the great town of Lone Hollow has to offer."

"I think we should get Miss Smith back to the ranch," Mr. Hemlock said. He yanked on the waistband of his pants, adjusting them. "The picnic might be too much for her.

"Says you." Benjamin elbowed his son in the stomach. "I want to stay, and I think Emma should stay too. I think it would do her good to get to know the people of Lone Hollow."

"Why? She's not from here." Mr. Hemlock shrugged and waved his hand slightly as though the movement proved whatever point he wished to make.

"I still think it will be good for her. Plus, getting outside and being in the fresh air can't be bad either. We're staying, and that's all there is to it, so don't think about arguing with me." Benjamin moved over to Emma and held his arm out for her to take. "Shall we, Emma?" A smile beamed across his face.

"We shall."

By the time they made it outside, the yard around the church was buzzing with people. Whether they were standing around chatting with one another or nibbling at one of the many tables laden with food, the smiles, and laughter both warmed Emma's chest in a comforting way and yet brought a slight sense of panic. She knew all of two people here.

Well, three, she thought, including the pastor in her list of known people.

She tightened her grip on Benjamin's arm, and he glanced at her, patting her hand. "Nervous?"

"Perhaps a little."

"Don't worry. Everyone will welcome you just fine. Are you hungry?"

Although her stomach had twisted itself into knots, it also growled with her thoughts of food, and she nodded.

"Then that is where we shall go." Benjamin patted her hand and arm again as he led her off to the table. A slight grunt from Mr. Hemlock echoed behind them.

~

JASPER

Jasper had never been one for many town functions. Of course, it didn't help that he missed most of them being on the stagecoach. When one is gone for more days and weeks out of the year than they are home, it's easy to distance oneself from the rest of the world. It wasn't that he didn't like people or wish to be in their company, but life on the road was just . . . easier.

Being home these last few weeks had changed so much, and while Jasper wanted to fight every moment of it, he couldn't help but pause from that knee-jerk reaction. He couldn't deny that it had been nice to be around Pa again. He had missed the old man and had missed not only his jokes and his pancakes, but he missed the company. He'd always been close with his parents, and he knew he needed to do more than just come home for a few days, only to leave again after his ma died.

The problem was putting that practice into place.

Although he loved his Pa and loved the idea of being around more, he also loved being on the stagecoach, riding around, and seeing the countryside as though he didn't have a care in the world.

It was a life he missed just as much being home, but it was also a life that, when taken away, opened his eyes to things he hadn't thought about. And, of course, the arrival of Miss Smith hadn't helped much either.

While he couldn't say anything wrong about the woman, a small part of him wanted to, and he didn't know why. She was, in truth, a lovely woman. Beautiful. Kind. Someone that seemed easy to speak to, and while she couldn't remember a lick of her past, she seemed content with it. As though nothing in the world could or would ever phase her. Jasper had known his fair share of women in his life from driving the stagecoach. He could always tell which ones were going to be trouble, whether they complained about the smell of the horses or the dust coming in the windows or whether they gave him hundreds of instructions on how to handle and pack their luggage. High maintenance, he always used to see them as, and having only known those types, he couldn't deny that Miss Smith hadn't been like that. She'd been pleasant and had taken everything with a sense that she could handle it no matter what.

He liked that about her.

And it was this thought that stopped him in his tracks.

He didn't want to like a woman.

Or did he?

With a hard 'no' to his thoughts, he shook his head, following the two of them over to a nearby table, where they all grabbed a plate and filled it with an assortment of treats.

"What did you think of the service today, Emma?" Pa asked the woman.

"I thought it was lovely. Something that even I could ponder and reflect on given my situation."

"Pastor Duncan is a wonderful pastor. He's always leaving me with that same thought each week. Like the sermon is so relatable, and I should pray about it. Do you remember anything about going to church? Any memories sparked when you were listening?"

"No." She shook her head. "I'd like to think that I went to church, but I can't remember."

"Well, Jasper and I would love for you to join us while you are staying with us."

"I would love that."

Jasper watched the two as he piled beans and cornbread onto his plate. While part of him wanted to disagree as he had every other time it was mentioned that Miss Smith go anywhere with them, a more significant part of him didn't mind her company, and that part stopped him from saying anything.

"Good afternoon, Jasper," a voice said behind him. He spun to find Cullen and Maggie McCray making their way toward them. Sadie, Cullen's niece, trotted alongside them, and Maggie held their tiny, new daughter in her arms.

"Cullen. Maggie," he said, nodding to them. "Good afternoon to you too."

"How have you been feeling? Is the wound healing all right?" Cullen asked.

"It's taking its time, but yes, I'm feeling better every day."

"That's good. I bet you will be able to return to the stagecoach soon."

"Yes, I hope to."

"I thought you liked being at home," Pa said, moving up alongside his son. He elbowed him in the waist and chuckled as though to say he was joking more than being serious.

Jasper glanced at the old man. "Well, I would if you would learn to cook."

"Perhaps Emma and I will just cook for ourselves from now

on, and you can go see about getting your supper from Boots every night."

"Emma?" Maggie cocked her head to the side and her brow furrowed.

Pa ducked his chin, then brushed his hand on his pants and turned slightly, motioning for Miss Smith to join them. "My apologies, Maggie. Cullen. May I introduce you to Miss Emma Smith? She's a guest staying with us out on the ranch for a while."

Miss Smith reached out, shaking the married couple's hands. "It's a pleasure to meet you."

"The pleasure is ours; I assure you," Maggie said. "We didn't know you were entertaining company, Jasper. Must be quite the change out there at the ranch." Maggie winked at him, and he ducked his chin again as warmth spread through his cheeks.

His bachelor status was always no secret around the town, and it was also no secret that Pa often asked the women of the town if they knew of a young lady looking for a husband.

"Miss Smith was involved in the stagecoach accident not far from town. Unfortunately, she lost her memories in the accident, and Dr. Miller thought it best she stayed someplace where she was comfortable. He's hopeful that she will heal, and her memories will return."

"Oh, my. I'm so sorry you have gone through such an ordeal." Maggie moved over to Ms. Smith, and she reached out with one hand, rubbing Miss Smith's arm. A crease formed in her brow once more, only this time it was out of concern, not confusion.

"Thank you."

"It must be such a shock. I don't know what I would do in that situation."

"It has. But Benjamin and Mr. Hemlock have been so gracious. It has been such a blessing."

While the two women continued to chat with their heads

close together, Cullen rested his hand on Jasper's shoulder, squeezing it.

"That's quite the thing to do for the woman. You're a good man, Jasper."

Pa let out a breath, letting it flutter his lips. "He fought the doc tooth and nail to put her up the in the hotel."

"I did not. I only suggested it once. But then I agreed to let her stay."

Pa waved his hand and rolled his eyes. "You've done nothing but try to get rid of that woman from the day you brought her home. And I know exactly why you have."

"Oh? And why is that?"

"Because you're scared of her. She's perfect, and you don't want to admit that she's perfect because if you did, you wouldn't be able to argue with the fact that I think it's about time you found yourself a wife, settled down, and started a family for yourself."

Cullen chuckled, giving Jasper's shoulder another squeeze. "I know how you feel. I was in the same situation when I met Maggie, and now look at us."

"Life on the road is different for a driver, and I don't want a wife or children. I'm tired of talking about it." A groan vibrated through Jasper's chest. However, along with it came a thought he didn't want to admit. The one who told him there was a chance he wasn't just lying to everyone else, but he was also lying to himself.

He glanced over toward Miss Smith as Maggie handed her the sleeping infant. A twinge of something he couldn't put his finger on twisted in his gut as he saw Miss Smith holding the child, and he shook his head, looking down at the plate of food in his hands. Suddenly, he wasn't as hungry as he was moments ago.

"She's beautiful," he heard Miss Smith say, and he glanced back up at her, thinking that he could say the same about her.

"She loves it when I sing to her, but I cannot carry a tune to save my life." Maggie laughed, brushing her fingers along her forehead.

"Singing, huh?" Miss Smith looked up toward Maggie then down at the infant. She opened her mouth and began to sing. Her voice was so stunning that it stopped everyone around her.

EIGHT

ELSA (EMMA)

Emma sat in the back of the wagon, watching the trees pass by. It was a warm afternoon, where the sun was already high and bright in the sky, radiating heat even through the tree branches.

"I still can't believe they asked her to sing," Mr. Hemlock glanced over at Benjamin as he drove the wagon.

Benjamin returned his look, then glanced over his shoulder, smiling at Emma. "I can believe it. Did you not hear her voice? It's the prettiest voice I've ever heard, and I'm an old man."

"But to ask a stranger to sing at your wedding? Doesn't that seem odd to you?" Mr. Hemlock tapped the reins on the horse's back, and the animal obliged the command, picking up a slight trot.

"No, I don't think it does." Benjamin glanced over his shoulder. "Do you think it was odd that Harrison and Amelia asked you to sing at their wedding, Emma?"

She had asked herself this question several times since last Sunday afternoon after church when the couple had asked her. As with most of the townsfolk at the church, they had overheard her singing to the baby and stopped what they were doing to listen to her.

"I don't know what I think," she answered.

"See?" Mr. Hemlock hooked his thumb over his shoulder, motioning toward her. "Even she thinks it's odd."

"She didn't say that." Benjamin glared at his son for a moment, then turned in his seat to face her. "Don't listen to him or anyone else. I'm not surprised they asked you, and I don't think it's odd. No one in this town has a voice like yours, and I know you will make their ceremony special."

"I just hope I can do a good job."

"I know you will."

They continued down the lane toward town and the small white schoolhouse at its edge. Townsfolk had already begun to gather for the wedding, and they meandered around, chatting with one another while dressed in their Sunday best. A sense of happiness and love seemed to dwell in everyone, though Emma supposed that was just because they were attending a wedding. Was there nothing more romantic than two people getting married?

Emma glanced down at her hands. She wasn't found with a ring on her finger, but that didn't mean there wasn't a man out there wondering where she was. Did she have a courted beau? Or had no one made their interest in her known? She wanted to remember, yet nothing she did helped bring back any memories.

Mr. Hemlock pulled the horse to a stop and climbed down, tying the reins on a line with the rest of the horses and wagons as Benjamin jumped down from his seat and helped Emma down from hers.

"We should find Amelia to let her know you are here," Benjamin said.

He laid his hand on the small of her back, leading her off to the schoolhouse while Mr. Hemlock headed in the other direction toward the crowd of people who were starting to take their seats set around the site where the ceremony would take place.

Emma glanced over her shoulder, meeting his gaze for a moment. The two of them smiled at one another, and for the first time, she wondered why he wasn't married. Did he not want a Mrs. Hemlock or not want children of his own? Had he been married, but she died? She knew nothing of his story, and while that wasn't surprising as he was a stranger, she still found herself asking questions and wondering what the answers were.

Benjamin knocked on the schoolhouse door, and after hearing Amelia tell them to come in, he opened it and guided Emma inside. Amelia sat at a desk in the corner, pinning her hair, and she glanced at them as Benjamin shut the door behind them.

"Oh, good. You are here," she said to Emma.

"Of course. You asked me to sing, so that is what I will do. Did you have a particular song in mind?"

"Well, I thought you could sing Amazing Grace as I walked down the aisle. I'm sure you know it."

"Yes, I do, and I think that would be lovely."

The two women smiled at one another, and Emma noticed one of Amelia's flowers in her hair had twisted and fallen to one side.

"Let me fix your flower." She moved toward the bride and lifted her hands, adjusting the bloom and the pin holding it in place.

"Thank you. I thought I should bring a mirror, but the one I have is too large for me to carry. I had to rely on that one." She motioned toward a hand-held mirror lying on the desk. The corner of the reflective glass had a crack in it, making it smaller than it already was.

"There. That's better."

"Thank you." Amelia heaved a sigh. "Have you seen it out there? Are there a lot of people?"

"Looks like most of the town. Although, I don't know how big the town is. But yes, there looks to be a lot of people."

"Poor Harrison. He had hoped it would have been just us like the sheriff and his wife, Cora. I just couldn't get married without the children around us, and the parents come with the children." She chuckled to herself with her joke.

"I'm sure that you two will have a lovely wedding no matter how many or how few guests are in attendance."

"Thank you." Amelia turned and grabbed the mirror, holding it up as she inspected the flowers. "It was twisted, wasn't it. Now it's perfect." She gave herself the once-over once more and turned back to face Emma. "I can't believe the day has finally arrived. It feels like we've been planning it forever."

"I can imagine most brides feel that way."

"Have you ever thought of marriage?"

"I'm sure I have. I mean, not recently, of course, but I'm sure I have. Perhaps."

"I'm sorry for the question. I shouldn't have asked it."

"No, it's all right." Emma smiled, hoping that Amelia would be comforted with it and not think she'd asked something she shouldn't. The question didn't upset Emma in any way, and she wanted to make sure Amelia knew it. "I'm sure I have thought of it, as I believe now that marriage is a lovely idea. I'm not sure what my life holds without my memories or if I will get them back or not. So, I'm not thinking of it now." Emma giggled at her tiny joke. "But hopefully, one day, I can. We shall see."

Amelia reached out, rubbing Emma's arm with her hand. "Well, I hope you find a man as wonderful as Harrison when the time does come for you."

"I hope so too."

The two women stared at one another, smiling until Benjamin cleared his throat. "We should get Emma outside so she can find her place and get ready."

"Oh, yes, we should. I can't be late for my own wedding.

Even if I was late to school the morning after Harrison and I met." She seemed to laugh at her memory then she waved her hands. "I'll be out a few minutes after you. Just start singing when you see me."

"I will."

Benjamin offered Emma his arm again, and he smiled at her as they left the church and headed toward the ceremony. All of the guests had already taken their seats and waited for Amelia to make her appearance.

"You know, my son is a wonderful man," Benjamin whispered as they strolled toward the ceremony site.

"And just what is that supposed to mean?"

"Oh, nothing. I was just mentioning it." He winked at her. "In case you were wondering."

Although he tried to be coy with his words, waving them off with a chuckle as though it was just as he said, something he was just mentioning, she knew that wasn't the case.

"I would think Mr. Hemlock already has a lady in mind should he desire to marry, or perhaps he doesn't desire it at all."

"Nah." Benjamin's word was more of a sound than an actual word, and he scrunched one side of his face. "I think he just is trying to ignore what he doesn't want to admit."

"Which is?"

"That he does want to marry, and he does want a family."

"Well, then perhaps when the time comes, he meets a nice young lady that suits him, he will."

Benjamin glanced at her and smiled. "Perhaps he already has and doesn't know it."

Emma opened her mouth to respond, but with the crowd closer to them, she shut it before she could utter a word. No one needed to overhear their conversation. Not when even she didn't want to be involved in it. She couldn't think of love or a husband right now. She didn't even know her own name! Just what this older man was thinking, she didn't know. Of course, she knew he meant well, and his choice of words was coming from a genuinely heartfelt place. It was just not something she could think about right now.

He led her down the aisle toward Pastor Duncan and Harrison, who were waiting. She smiled at them both, and as Benjamin left to take his seat, she turned toward the crowd. The sudden view of dozens and dozens of faces hit her like a stone, and she sucked in a breath. A memory of a theater, lights, and a cheering crowd flashed in her mind.

She had sung before a crowd before.

Many times.

~

JASPER

Jasper sat in his seat, watching Miss Smith standing in front of the crowd. Her eyes widened, and she sucked in a breath, looking as though something was wrong. For a moment, he wondered if he should do something, but before he could even think to move, she seemed to calm, exhaling a deep breath before she began her tune.

Although he'd heard Amazing Grace tens of dozens of times in his life, he hadn't heard it sung the way she sang it. The notes were so perfect, and her voice hit the keys as though the song was written just for her to sing it.

She did have the most beautiful voice he'd heard, and by the time she finished, all he wanted was for her to continue.

After finishing the song, she bowed her head, nodding toward the couple as the townsfolk applauded. A slight pinkness blushed through her cheeks, and as she made her way over to the seat Pa had saved for her, her face seemed to warm with an even brighter color. He wanted to stand and hug her, and the thought of his urge caught him off guard.

A hug, what was he, nuts, he asked himself.

Obviously, he was suffering from some sort of delusion if he had such a thought as hugging the woman go through his mind.

He shook his head and dropped his gaze to his lap as he tried to ignore how as Miss Smith approached, Pa moved over into the seat next to the one he saved for her, sitting her next to Jasper instead.

Did this man know no boundaries?

Her eyes widened as she took her seat and glanced over at Jasper. Her movement caught his eye, and as he met her gaze, he noticed her lungs were heaving. And he got the feeling it wasn't from the singing.

"What's the matter?" he whispered as he leaned in closer to her. The light scent of her perfume brushed against his nose, and for a slight second, he wanted to get lost in it.

Focus, Jasper, he thought.

"I remembered something. I have sung in front of people before. I think I'm a singer. A singer from a big city."

"The only big city around is Butte."

"Does that mean I'm from Butte?"

"I don't know. But we can find out."

NINE

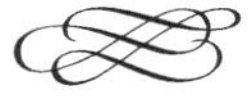

JASPER

Although Jasper had sent a telegram to the sheriff in Butte about any missing young ladies who were singers and was hopeful they would hear good news, he also couldn't deny a tiny part of him wasn't sure he was ready to listen to the answer. No matter how long or how short of time it would take to hear back. And it was these thoughts and feelings that confused him more than anything he's ever known.

"Have you heard back from the sheriff in Butte?" Pa asked as he threw the straps of the cinch over the horse's back. Jasper buckled it and attached the other end to the wagon hitch.

"Not yet."

"Well, maybe we will hear something when we return from the county fair."

"Yeah. Maybe." Jasper's brow furrowed as he spoke. He wanted to look forward to the fair. Or at least had looked forward to it until all this happened. Now all he could think about was the possibility of figuring out who Miss Smith was and that when they did, she would be leaving his ranch and leaving Lone Hollow.

"You sound as though you don't want the sheriff to respond."

"And what is that supposed to mean?"

"I don't know. It just seems like you don't want the sheriff to respond because you don't want Emma to leave."

His head whipped toward Pa. "Are you out of your ever-lovin' mind? What kind of a statement is that?"

Pa held up his hands. "I was only telling you what I've noticed."

"Well, whatever you think you see or believe you know about the situation is wrong. So, just stop thinking it's anything like you are. It's nothing. I'm hoping the sheriff does find out who she is so she can return to where she belongs."

The guest house door shut behind him, and he spun to see Miss Smith standing on the porch, looking at them as they prepared the wagon so they could go to the county fair.

~

Jasper pulled the wagon up to the fair and parked it with the other wagons. All three of them climbed down, and while Jasper and Pa went to work, unloading all the supplies, Emma watched.

"What do you need all this for?" she asked.

"For Jasper's County Famous chili that he enters in the cook-off every year."

"You have famous chili?" she asked Jasper.

A slight blush warmed through his cheeks, and he shrugged. "I don't know if I would say it's that famous."

"It's won more blue ribbons than any other chili in the county," Benjamin said. "I guess that's my son, though, modest to a fault." The older man continued grabbing wood from the wagon before he heaved several chunks up onto his shoulders and trudged off toward a crowd of people.

Emma watched him until he disappeared, then she turned to Jasper, who was still unloading supplies.

"So, are you going to show me how to make this famous chili?" she asked him.

He smiled and cocked his head to the side, closing one eye as though he wanted to show he was hesitating. It wasn't in a mean manner, though, but was more in a playful way that made her chuckle. "I don't know. If I show you what is to stop you from stealing my recipe?"

"Well, I guess I could give you my word."

"Trusting the word of a stranger? It seems risky."

"You could show me without telling me what you're putting in it."

"That's an idea I like a little more."

"Or you could just show me everything, and I could secretly write it down, copying the recipe so I can show it to the whole country, sending it to different newspapers for everyone to know."

"And we are back to not liking the idea at all."

They both laughed, and as he calmed, he cocked his head to the side. "I suppose I can trust you enough to show you. For all I know, you may not like it."

"That's true. I could think it was the most disgusting thing I've ever eaten." She stepped forward, holding her arms out. "Now, hand me some of the wood so I can help."

"Yes, ma'am."

~

By the time they reached the fire pit near the booth space for the chili cook-off contestants, most of the other entrants were already busy chopping up onions and peppers and adding them to their mixtures hanging over the fire. The first year that Jasper had entered the contest, the sight of everyone already at work made him nervous, as though he was doing something wrong by not having the chili going already by the crack of dawn. Over the years, however, he learned it was all right. That his recipe didn't call for hours and hours of cooking, and while he always wondered if it would taste better if he did, he hadn't ever been brave enough to deviate from the way he did things.

"Why don't you go fetch the water, and I'll start chopping?" Benjamin glanced over his shoulder as he picked up a couple of buckets and handed them to Emma before picking up another bucket and giving it to Jasper.

Jasper nodded and motioned her to follow him.

"Where do we get the water from?" she asked.

Jasper glanced at her, then at a man busy cooking his chili as they passed him. "We get it down at the river," he said loudly.

She cocked one eyebrow, staring at him for a moment but didn't say anything until they were out of earshot from anyone near the fair.

"So, where do we really get the water?"

"What do you mean?"

"Don't think I didn't notice how you answered my question. Raising your voice so that man heard you on purpose."

"You're perceptive." He glanced over and smiled at her. "And you're right. I'll let you on a secret."

"Which is?"

"While everyone gets their water from the creek, I go across the creek to a spring hidden in the trees. Of course, this spring feeds into the creek, but it mixes with the lake runoff, which is the main source of the creek through the town."

"And no one else knows about this spring?"

"A few people do. But I don't think the other ones in the contest are any of them that do. Either that or they don't believe it makes a difference in the chili."

"But you think it does?"

"Oh, I know it does."

As they reached the creek, he glanced over his shoulder, ensuring that no one was around or was watching them.

"Follow me," he said.

Before she could respond, he hopped on several rocks to cross the creek and then waited for Miss Smith to do the same, watching her as she stepped on the same stones and steadied her balance as she reached the others side. Once she made it, they continued through the trees, ducking low in the bushes for several yards before coming to a small clearing where the water bubbled up from the ground.

He bent down, removed a glass from his pocket, and used it to scoop up the water. "The only problem is that getting it in the buckets takes longer," he said, pouring the water into the bucket.

"I can see that."

"Here." He reached into his other pocket, yanking out a second glass he thought to bring for her. "Start filling this up and then dump it in the bucket."

She crossed over the spring, kneeling on the other side before she began filling the glass and dumping it in the bucket.

"So, you think this makes a difference?"

"Well, why don't you taste it and see for yourself."

She cocked her head to the side but smiled and filled the glass before taking it to her lips for a gulp. A bigger smile spread across her face after taking a sip, and she blinked as though she was in a state of disbelief.

"Wow. That is amazing. It's so cold and the taste . . ."

"I know."

"It's not like any water I've ever had."

"That's what you get from a natural spring. I wish I had one on the ranch, but I have yet to find one."

"Well, I can see how this would make chili better. It would make anything better." She paused for a moment, and her brow furrowed a little.

"What's the matter?"

"It's just that . . . I never knew things like this existed. I mean, yes, I know I don't have all of my memories, but I have remembered so much else, like what animals are or trees." She glanced up at the branches hanging over their heads. "But still, with all that I remember, this isn't a part of that. I never knew springs like this were real."

"And that's a problem?"

"I don't know if I would call it that. But it makes me wonder about my life. Like was I happy before the accident? Did I enjoy being a singer? If I was, that is. Did I have money? Did I care only for that money and for nothing else?" She ducked her head for a moment as though she wanted to continue her questions and yet didn't at the same time. She sucked in a breath, holding it for a moment before exhaling it. "I have so many questions, and I hate that most of them are about the worst parts of me. Like was I a shallow person?"

"Do you think you were?"

"I don't know. I mean, I'd like to think that I wasn't, but I don't know. I want to know who I was, but I'm scared to know at the same time." With her words finally out, she tucked her chin down, resuming the work of filling the bucket.

He stared at her for a while, watching her continue to fill the bucket. He felt as though it had been an admission she didn't know if she could make, and even though she'd made it anyway, she didn't know how she felt about it. It was a moment of utter vulnerability and one he hadn't seen in anyone before. Especially himself. While he had always looked at her with a hint of pity, he couldn't do that anymore. Instead, he looked upon her with pride, and he almost envied her that she could be so honest with themselves out loud to another person.

"That probably sounds silly to you," she said, snorting a breath from her nose.

"No, it doesn't. It makes sense, and I can understand why you would be concerned. But I also think that while you can't change who you were in the past, you can change who you are in the future. Should you find out it wasn't someone you wish to be."

"That's true. I just get this feeling that I was lonely, and after being in this town and with you and your father . . . I don't know if I could return to a lonely life."

A lump formed in his throat as he thought of so many things he could say. Of course, they all sounded stupid, and while he wanted to know why, he didn't. They just felt stupid.

"Yeah. I can understand how you feel," he finally said, half regretting his words and hoping they brought her comfort—even if it was only a little.

She glanced up at him, and their eyes met for a moment. She looked as though she wanted to say something else; however, she didn't. She only smiled then went back to work, filling her buckets one glassful of spring water at a time.

~

In the time they'd been gone, Pa had already built and lit the fire and had hanged the pot over the flames. Miss Smith and Jasper poured the buckets of water in, and while Pa grabbed two of the buckets and took off in the direction of the creek.

"Is he going back for more water? Did we not get enough?" Miss Smith asked.

"No, we didn't. This will be enough to start the chili, but as it simmers sometimes, we need more. We take it back to the ranch and drink it if we don't use it." He winked at her, and she giggled at the inside joke.

"So, what can I help you with now?" she asked.

"We need to pour in the jars of soaked beans from the crate, then cut up the meat, onions, and peppers so we can add those in."

Before he could say anything else, she darted over to the crates, grabbing the jars of beans and handing him some while she grabbed the rest. They both moved over to the pot, unscrewing the lids of each jar before dumping the beans into the pot. The spring water they had poured in first was already starting to steam and get hot and a bit splattered on his arm as he emptied the jars of beans into it.

"Do we move on to the chopping now?" she asked.

"Yes."

"All right. I'll take the vegetables, and you take the meat?"

"Sounds good."

While he hesitated for a moment, she darted back to the crates, grabbing the onions and peppers before moving to the cutting board. She plunged a knife into one of the onions, working at the outer layers, and as she sniffed back her tears from the pungent smell, he couldn't help but hold onto the bit of amusement that warmed through his chest. He hadn't wanted to admit that he wasn't ready for her to learn who she was. It wasn't because he didn't want her to know or wished to keep her from finding out—for that would be cruel. But it was because he wasn't ready for her to leave him.

TEN

ELSA (EMMA)

Emma wiped her hands together, wishing the movement would wipe away the smell of the onions. Her eyes still stung, but the more she blinked, the more her tears seemed to calm them, and by the time she scooped the bits of onion and peppers into the pot of chili, they were pretty much free of pain.

"Is that enough?" she asked Mr. Hemlock.

"Yes, it is. Now all I have to do is add the meat." He sliced the slab of beef a few more times then dumped the chunks into the pot. "And, of course, add in the secret stuff, and we should be done. All it has to do is simmer for a few hours."

She leaned in, dropping her voice to a whisper. "What is the secret stuff?"

"Well, first of all, it's pork."

"Pork? As in more meat?"

"Yes, the bacon cut of it. I chop up the bacon and add it in."

"And that's what makes it win every year?"

"Well, that and some spices and herbs that Boot's gives me."

"I see. And no one has thought to add in pork, too?"

"Not that I know of." He glanced around them as though he

was making sure no one was listening to their conversation. "Even if anyone did, they still wouldn't have the blend of herbs and spices I use."

"I didn't think making chili was such a . . . passion around here."

"Well, it only is with certain townsfolk. Most don't care. They just like eating it." He dumped the last chunks of meat into the pot then stirred it with a big spoon before taking a huge whiff. "I think it's time just to let it simmer."

"So, now what we do?" she asked, glancing around.

"Now, you two go and enjoy the fair." Benjamin's voice boomed behind them, and as Emma spun to face him, he met her with a smile. "I mean it. Go on, you two. I'll look after the chili."

"But you know it has to be stirred—"

"Stirred every so often or else it won't cook properly. I know. I've only seen you make this chili about a hundred times." He waved his hands. "Now, go. Have fun. Enjoy the fair and show Emma all the things she can do."

He flicked his wrists, walking toward them as though to shoo them off. They both followed his orders, and Emma followed Mr. Hemlock away from the fire pit and toward the different crowds and lines of people enjoying themselves. While she didn't know for sure if she'd ever been to a county fair, taking the sights of this one, she doubted she had. Surely, she would have remembered such a time.

Men, women, and children wandered all around her, heading toward different booths.

"What do you want to do?" Mr. Hemlock asked.

"I . . . I don't know."

"Do you want to check out the games?"

"Sure."

She followed him over to one of the first booths. Several bottles were lined in the middle, and a few men stood around the edge, tossing iron rings at the tops of the bottles. They all missed, and while a few of them gave up and walked away after a few tries, a couple paid more money to get more chances.

"What do they get when they win, Mr. Hemlock?" she asked him.

He smiled at her. "I think one of those." He pointed toward a bear made of material with two buttons for eyes and stitched up the middle. "And you may call me Jasper. You don't have to keep calling me Mr. Hemlock."

"Oh. All right. I suppose if we are on a first-name basis . . ."

"Then I shall call you Emma."

She nodded as heat flushed up the back of her neck and around to her cheeks. She looked away, praying they weren't as pink as they felt hot. Even though Emma wasn't her real name, the way it rolled off his lips sent her stomach fluttering. She didn't want to think about how her real name would sound.

"So, Emma, shall I try to win you one of those . . . stuffed bears?"

"If you want to, but you don't have to."

"Of course, I have to. I suppose I shouldn't have even asked." He chuckled to himself as he dug into his pocket and yanked out some money. "Good, Sir." He motioned toward the man standing near the bottles. "I would like to try."

The man made his way over to them and smiled. "Yes, Sir. It's two cents for three rings."

"Two cents, huh? Well." Jasper looked down at the coins in his hand. "Give me ten cents worth."

The man blinked at him. "You . . . you want ten cents worth?"

"Yep." He handed the man a dime, and the man counted the rings, handing them over to Jasper before he tipped his hat. "Good luck."

Jasper stepped back and began tossing the rings toward the tops of the bottles. One by one, they would hit the tops; the sound pinged as they not only hit the bottle but then landed somewhere in between them. Each time he missed, he would hiss then try again, either changing his stance or closing one eye —as though it made him aim better. With only two rings left, he tossed the third to the last, and it landed on one of the bottles, spinning in circles as it settled around the neck. He lifted his arms in victory as she clapped.

"You did it," she said to him.

"Which one would you like, Sir?" the man asked him, pointing to the bears.

"Which one?" he asked her.

She looked over them and pointed toward a darker brown one with tan buttons for eyes. "That one."

"Then that one it is." The man untied it from a board and handed it to her. "There you go. Congratulations."

"Thank you." She took the bear from the man, studying it. A smile spread across her face, and she looked at Jasper. "Thank you for winning the bear."

"You're welcome." He reached out as though to ask for the bear, and after she gave it to him, he glanced over it and handed it back. "It's probably the cutest ten cents I've ever spent."

They both laughed.

"What do you want to do next?" he asked.

"I don't know. What would you suggest?"

"Are you hungry?"

"No, not yet."

"Well, we could see one of the shoot-out shows."

'What is that?"

He opened his mouth but shut it and waved his hand. "I'll take you there and show you. It will be better than trying to explain."

He led her over toward a crowd that encircled a stage. A man was standing on the stage, talking to those watching, asking them questions about news events around the country. The subject turned to types of guns, and then, finally, he asked if anyone wanted to take part in the bets to see who would win. Dozens around them lifted their hands, waving dollar bills in the air as they shouted their answers and bets. Different men walked through the crowds, taking the money from those who wanted to bet and writing their answers.

The sound around them almost deafened her, and yet, no matter how loud the crowd got, she loved every minute of it. It felt like everyone around her lived their lives to the fullest. Exciting. Pulsing.

Once the bets were taken, the men returned behind the stage, and two other men joined the one still speaking. They had guns holstered to their waists, and as they waved to the crowd, the men who were taking the bets came out, carrying targets that they set up on the other end of the stage.

"What are those for?"

"For the men to shoot at. Whoever gets the best shot, the one closest to the bullseye . . . see it in the middle?"

"Yes."

"They will try to shoot as close to the bullseye as possible. Whoever does, wins."

She glanced from the targets to the men a few times, and while she was sizing up the scene, a few men moved in front of her, blocking her view. She lifted on her toes, shifting from side to side to help her see. A few more men moved in front of her, and she stepped over to the left, hoping for a better view. The sudden space between her and Jasper seemed like a perfect opportunity for people to move themselves to get a better view, and within just a few seconds, they were separated in the crowd.

"Emma? Emma?"

She heard Jasper call out her name several more times, and as she turned to see him, she couldn't find him. He wasn't anywhere.

"Jasper?" she yelled.

He called back to her, but she still couldn't see him no matter how many times she heard his voice. They called to each other while she continued to search for him. Weaving in and out of the crowd, people bumped into her from one side and the other. Some growled as though annoyed she was there, while others tipped their hats and smiled.

Her heart thumped harder with each second that she couldn't see him, and the more the man on the stage spoke, and the two shooters prepared to shoot at the target, the crowd pressed in on each other as though everyone wanted to get closer to the stage for a better view.

"Jasper?" she called out again.

A shot rang out, and the sound of the gun firing vibrated through her chest. It made her flinch, and she whipped around to face the stage. Another shot rang out. She flinched again. Her breathing quickened.

"Emma?" a voice shouted to her left, and as she turned, Jasper weaved his way toward her. He heaved a deep sigh. "There you are. Are you all right?"

"Yes." Another gunshot rang out, and she flinched again.

"Why don't we do something else? Do you want to see the animals?"

"Animals?"

"People all over the county raise pigs, goats, sheep, and cows, and they are judged. Some of the animals are nice. I've always wanted to bid on one in the auction, but I can't bring myself to do it." He motioned her to go ahead of him through the crowd, and he pressed his hand on the small of her back as though he was trying to guard her and didn't want to lose her again.

"Why don't you bid on them?" she asked as they were finally clear of the crowd.

"Because I got no use for a show animal. What do I care if the pigs I eat came from a prize-winning pig?" He chuckled at his joke. "Or the milk I drink came from a cow who won a blue ribbon?"

"I guess I understand that."

They continued toward the far corner of the fair. The closer they neared the pens with the animals, the thinner the crowd became. Sure, some wanted to gawk over the farm creatures, but most picked the games, food, and entertainment shows if given a choice.

"Mr. Hemlock?" a voice called out. "Miss Smith?"

They both turned to see Harrison and Amelia waving at them, and they made their way over to the pen where the newlywed couple was standing.

"What are you doing here, Mr. Craig?" Jasper asked.

"Well, the wife . . . that's still odd to say . . . anyway, the wife and I had a stellar crop of rabbits this year, so we thought we would bring them to the fair to auction them off." Harrison hooked this thumb toward the makeshift pen of rabbits and Amelia standing in the middle of it. A broad grin spread across her face, and she waved at Emma to join her.

"It's good to see you," she said as Emma approached.

"It's good to see you, too. How have you been?"

"Couldn't be better."

Rabbits hopped all around their feet, and Amelia bent down, grabbing one of them. She hoisted it up, holding it in her arms.

"You have a lot of rabbits in here," Emma said, laughing.

"I know. They seem to have exploded overnight. It was like we went to bed with ten and woke up to a hundred. Perhaps even more. I hope they sell. It was hard enough getting here with all of them. I don't want to take them all home."

"I don't blame you. But they are cute." Emma reached over and stroked the head of the rabbit in Amelia's arms.

"Oh, if you think this one is cute . . ." Amelia bent down, setting the rabbit back onto the dirt. It hopped away a few feet, then turned to look at her as if to protest her dumping it for someone else. "Just come over here." Amelia wiggled her finger, and Emma followed her over to a box in the corner. "I can't tell you how much I hope no one takes them."

Emma peered down in the box at seven baby rabbits the size of a bar of soap. She gasped and slapped her hands against her cheeks. "Oh, my word. They are adorable."

"I know. And so friendly." Amelia bent down and grabbed two of them, handing one of them to Emma while she held onto the other one.

Emma's eyes misted with tears as she couldn't help but tear up at the soft cuteness in her arms. Of course, logic told her rabbits were small as babies. How could they not be given the size of them as adults, but to see how tiny they were in person . . . it was something she'd never thought about.

"I just can't believe how soft they are. How tiny." She glanced over at Jasper, who was still standing with Harrison. The two men had stopped their conversation to watch the women fawn over the baby rabbits, and Jasper smiled. "It's so little," she said to him.

Both men made their way over to the women, and as they approached, Harrison slapped Jasper on the back. "I'll make you a deal on all seven."

Jasper laughed. "No way. I'm not getting into rabbits. Pigs, cows, fine. Rabbits, not a chance."

"But they are so cute," Emma said to him.

"I know they are. But then, in a few months, you have to eat them."

"Eat them!" Emma's mouth gaped, and she looked around at all three of their faces.

"Haven't you ever had rabbit?" Harrison asked.

"Well, I don't know, but I'm pretty sure it wouldn't be my first choice." She glanced over at Amelia. Although she never would want to judge another woman, she couldn't help but wonder how it was so easy for her to sell these rabbits to people, knowing the people planned to kill them and eat them.

"Don't worry." Amelia laid her hand on Emma's shoulder. "I don't eat rabbit either, and although I hate the thought of other people eating them . . . well, I try not to think about it."

"I don't think I could either," Emma said. "I would just want one as a pet. Something to take with me everywhere I go."

"Like a dog?" Jasper held a slight chuckle at the thought.

"Yes, like a dog. If I had a proper crate for it, I mean. Why not have a pet rabbit?"

"I suppose it wouldn't be hard." Jasper scratched his chin and snorted as though his thoughts amused him. "Well, Mr. Craig, how much for one of the babies?"

"For you or Miss Smith?"

"For Emma, of course."

Harrison slapped Jasper on the back. "I'm sure Amelia and I would agree she can have it."

"Are you serious?" Emma's gaze danced between the two.

"Of course. It's the least we could do after you sang so lovely at our wedding."

"Well, thank you. I don't know where I will put it, though."

Jasper stepped forward, looking down at the tiny rabbit as he stroked its head with his thumb. Its ears flattened against the top of its head from the touch, and it closed its eyes. "We can put it in one of the supply crates we brought for the chili fixings. It will be safe until we get it home. Then I'll build you something better."

He glanced up at her, and their eyes met.

"That sounds perfect," she said.

"I'm glad. Now, I hate to break up this happy moment, but we should probably get back to the chili."

She tucked the rabbit tight into her chest, protecting it with her hands. "Just lead the way."

ELEVEN

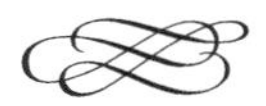

JASPER

Jasper tapped the reins on the horse's back. Although he was in a hurry to get home because he was tired and only wanted his bed, he couldn't deny that he rather enjoyed the time in the wagon with Emma sitting next to him. Even if they didn't talk, there was something about how she just sat next to him, not speaking as she cuddled with the rabbit and held onto his blue ribbon for winning first place for his chili again.

"Did you have fun?" he asked her.

She glanced over at him and nodded. Her movement caused her eyes to flutter, and she yawned.

"Tired?"

She nodded again. "I could probably fall asleep sitting in this wagon."

"Well, we don't have too far to go before we are back at the ranch."

"I don't think I will join you two for dinner. I think I'm just going to turn in for the night in the guesthouse."

"Oh. All right." Although he tried to hide it—and wanted to

believe he had—he feared his disappointment showed in his tone and his words.

They continued down the lane in silence, listening to the wagon wheels roll across the ground as the sun dipped farther and further toward the horizon. Chirps from the birds had vanished as the winged animals began settling into their nests to sleep for the night. While they took to their homes, the crickets and frogs awoke for the night, and the sounds of their excitement for the darkness echoed in the trees. Pa slept in the back of the wagon, and Jasper could hear his soft snores, his breathing rhythmic.

"Do you have a name for the rabbit?" he asked her, finally unable to take the silence.

"I'm not sure. I don't know if it's a boy or a girl, so I don't know what to call it."

"You could find a name that would fit either if you wanted to."

"Like what?"

"I don't know." He glanced at the ball of fur in her lap. "It's brown. What about Brownie?"

"That could work."

"Or Bunny."

"Bunny for a boy?"

"Yeah, you have a point." He laughed and glanced down at it again, noticing how fast the nose moved. "You know, their noses move like no other animals I know."

"What is your point?"

"Well, that's quite the overactive sniffer. What about Sniffer?"

"You know, I kind of like that. Although, it is rather odd."

"Eh, so it's odd. It's already odd to have a pet rabbit."

"That's true." She giggled and looked down at the tiny thing in her lap, stroking its whole body with one movement. "Sniffer it is."

"I'll build it a crate tomorrow, and you can keep it in the guest house. Then as it gets older, we can build a bigger hutch and pen for it outside."

"Do you think it will get lonely outside by itself?"

"Maybe. But if you tame it like I think you will, you'll have it in the guest house more often than not." He chuckled at the thought of a rabbit running around the house like a dog.

"Do you think I will be here long enough to build a hutch outside?" she asked. Although it seemed by her tone, she wanted to look at him; she didn't. Instead, she kept her gaze locked on the rabbit in her lap.

His stomach clenched with her question and even more with the answer that popped into his head. The truth of the matter, and the luck of the situation, told him that she wouldn't be, but to say the words was a lot different than just thinking them.

"Well, um, I don't know."

"Did the sheriff in Butte say anything about how long it would take to get back to you?"

"No. He didn't." Jasper cleared his throat. His stomach tightened even more.

"Oh. Well, I guess we shall see then."

"Yeah." His brow furrowed and a crease formed on his forehead. He cleared his throat a second time. "I can still make the crate for it, however. That way, you can take it with you."

"That would be helpful. Thank you."

They both fell silent, and there was an uncomfortable air between them as the wagon wheels continued down the lane.

"May I ask you something?" she asked.

"Of course."

"How did you become a stagecoach driver?"

He shrugged, falling back into a sea of memories of when his ma died and his pa became the hollow shell of a man he once was. Although Jasper had wanted to stay with him, he couldn't bear seeing him in the state he was in, and driving had been just the distraction he'd needed. What he had planned on was getting out of Lone Hollow for most of the month and coming home only when he had to. What he hadn't planned on was not only how much he loved it but how the work had suited him more than he thought it would.

"It's a long story. My ma passed away, and I . . . I just needed out of this town."

"I can understand that. Do you enjoy it?"

"I do. Although, the last few weeks being home . . . it's like I'm torn in two. One part of me wants to get back out there, driving through the countryside, sleeping under the stars. I'll tell you there is nothing like the night sky in the middle of a Montana prairie."

"Pretty, huh?"

"Just about the prettiest thing I've ever seen. Aside from one other sight." He wanted to look at her when he spoke, as he tried to convey the truth that it was her who he thought was the prettiest. However, he chickened out and focused on the horse pulling the wagon.

"And the other part of you?"

"I hate leaving Pa alone. It wasn't as bad a few years ago, but the time hasn't been kind. Hot summers, cold winters. Every time I've come home after a few weeks of traveling, he seems to age. I know he would disagree with me on that and tell me I was wrong or didn't know what I was talking about. But I do. I see it. I want to think he sees it, too. He's just too stubborn to admit it."

"What are you going to do?"

"I don't know. I've got to make a living, and yet, for what, I don't know. Not to mention, how am I going to feel when he's gone too, and I've missed all those years I could have been here."

"I don't think he would want you to miss out on your life because of him."

"No, I know he wouldn't, either. But . . . I don't think I'd be missing out on life if I was here with him. Does that make sense? How can you miss out on life if you're with people you love?"

"It makes sense." She heaved a deep breath. "I've been thinking a lot about whether or not there are people out there who love me and are missing me. I hate to admit this, but as much as I would like to say there are, something is holding me back from thinking there are. As though my gut is trying to tell me that there isn't anyone. I'm not sure how I feel about that."

"Does it bother you to think there isn't anyone?"

She turned her face toward him but stopped before fully facing him. She kept her gaze on the horse and hesitated while a crease formed on her forehead.

"Emma?"

"It does bother me. It bothers me to think I could be a singer who entertains people for a living but who had no one in her own life." She paused, biting her life. "It more than bothers me, honestly. It terrifies me."

He wanted to ignore how her voice cracked on the last of her words. He didn't know how he could take it if she started crying, but luckily, she straightened her shoulders and brushed her hair back, blinking as though she didn't want to cry in front of him any more than he wanted her to, either.

"I suppose in the end, though, all I can do is change. I can't change the past, but I can change the future. When I learn what that is."

"Yeah, that's true. I guess I can do that too. Maybe I won't travel as much. Take more time off. I don't exactly know how the stagecoach company will take the news. But I guess it doesn't matter."

"I'm sure Benjamin will enjoy the time with you."

"Yeah, or he'll just see it as more time to pester me about getting married and starting a family." As soon as the words left his lips, Jasper regretted them. They had come without warning, spewing from his mouth like an out-of-control train barreling down the tracks, and he cleared his throat and tapped the horse into a faster walk.

"May I ask you why you aren't married?" She bit her lip again. "I mean, if my asking doesn't offend you."

"No, it doesn't." His stomach flipped, and he tightened his grip on the reins. "I . . . I just don't know if I have an answer. I just haven't considered it, I guess."

"Never?"

"Well, maybe, a few times. I mean, who hasn't thought about it? Surely, you have." While part of him felt guilty for knocking the question back in her lap, the other part of him was so desperate to get the attention off of his reasons. A tiny twinge of guilt rested in his chest, and he ignored it.

"Oh, I don't know. I mean, perhaps I had. I certainly haven't thought of it recently, however. There is just far too much going on in my life right now. I don't even know my name."

"That's understandable."

She straightened her shoulders and tucked her chin down to her chest. "I apologize if I asked something I shouldn't have."

"No, you didn't." The tiny hint of guilt prickled with more intensity, and he closed his eyes for a moment, groaning under his breath so she wouldn't—at least he hoped—hear it. "The truth of the matter is I have considered it. But with my job and schedule . . . I'm just not home often enough, and the risk that is involved . . ." He glanced over and motioned toward his shoulder. "The accident that caused this could have been a lot worse. I don't want to leave a widow and orphans on this earth."

"I can understand that."

"I just don't think it would be fair to do that to a woman."

"It's a commendable thing to say and think. However, . . ." She let her voice trail off as she glanced out into the trees.

"However, what?"

"It's nothing. Forget I said anything."

"No. I won't. What do you mean by, however?"

"While it's a commendable thing to say, I can't help but wonder if it's more of an excuse than a reason."

His heart thumped. No matter how many times Pa had broached the subject with him, he'd never questioned him as she did, especially not with such a question she just asked. It wasn't that he didn't have an answer for it. It was that he did, but he didn't want to admit it. While he did believe his reason was a valid reason, a tiny part of him knew it was more of an excuse than anything. Sure, it wouldn't be right or fair to leave a woman a widow or children orphans—especially knowingly. But he also couldn't deny that he held onto that fear and proclamation probably a little tighter than he should. While his job was a risk, he could take steps to lessen that risk. No more long drives. No more overnight drives. He could request a different schedule and request a different route. Other men did this and had happy families and home lives.

"I apologize if I overstepped again," she said, studying his hesitation and silence. "I shouldn't have said anything."

"No, you don't have to apologize. You did nothing wrong. It's a valid question."

"And one, I feel you don't wish to answer."

"Is it that obvious?"

She laughed. "I don't know if I should tell you the truth now."

"Don't start holding out on me now when you've already said so much." They both chuckled, and he heaved a deep sigh as he shook his head. "I'm just happy Pa wasn't awake to hear this conversation."

"So, does that mean you're thinking a little more about marriage?"

His heart thumped again, and he didn't know if he wanted to answer or not. "I don't know, but I will give it some thought."

She glanced over at him and smiled, chuckling again as she

turned her gaze toward the trees and night sky around them. He both wanted and didn't want to know her thoughts, and although he expected her to continue, he wasn't surprised when she didn't. Truth be told, he was a little relieved when she didn't. He didn't need to think about how marriage and a family were all he'd thought about as of late.

Nor did he need to think about how he saw her face when he thought of a wife.

The ranch came into view as they turned around a corner, and as they neared the cabin, Jasper spied a man sitting on the porch in the rocking chair. He pulled the horse to a stop and jumped down, approaching Sheriff Bullock as the sheriff removed his hat.

"Evening, Sheriff," Jasper said.

"Evening, Jasper."

"What can I do for you tonight?"

"I got a telegram from the sheriff of Butte. It seems that a young woman by the name of Miss Elsa Crestwood has been reported as missing by her uncle, Mr. Clancy Bates. She's a singer at the Half Moon Theater in Butte."

Jasper sucked in a deep breath. "So . . . then Miss Smith is probably this Miss Crestwood."

"Yes, I believe so. The description of Miss Crestwood matches the description of Miss Smith."

Jasper's blood chilled in his veins. There hadn't been many times in his life when his knees felt weak under his weight. The first was when his ma died, and the second was when the bullet from the Bennett brother's gun hit him in the arm. He didn't want to think that this was the third time, even if it was.

"Oh. Well, I guess that's good news, then."

Sheriff Bullock cocked his head, giving a half-smile that vanished in a few seconds. "Are you sure? Because it doesn't sound as though you think it is."

"No. No." Jasper shook his head. "No, it is. I'll . . . I guess I'll go inform her."

Sheriff Bullock put his hat back on his head and tipped it. "Have a nice evening, Jasper."

"Thank you, and you, too, Sheriff Bullock."

Jasper walked back to the wagon as the sheriff made his way back to his horse, climbed on, and trotted away from the ranch. He smiled at Emma as her brow furrowed.

"Is everything all right?" she asked.

"Yeah. It seems Sheriff Bullock received a telegram from the sheriff in Butte."

"What did it say?"

While a small part of him didn't want to tell her, he knew he had to. And this knowledge churned in his stomach. He wasn't ready for her to leave and wasn't prepared to say goodbye.

"Well, it seems your real name is Miss Elsa Crestwood. You're a singer at the Half Moon Theater, and it was your uncle who reported you missing."

She sucked in a breath. "Oh. So, now what?"

"I guess now . . . we should get you to Butte. We can leave in the morning if you want."

"Yeah. I guess that will be all right." She slid over to the side of the wagon, and he helped her down. "I'll start packing."

"And I'll make sure everything is ready for us to leave. I have a crate you can use in the meantime for Sniffer. It should be all right until you get back in the city and can purchase something more suitable."

"All right." Her gaze danced around, and she bit her lip.

He wanted to tell her they could wait, that they didn't have to leave so fast, but he didn't. Instead, he smiled and nodded before striding off toward the barn, leading the horse and wagon behind him.

TWELVE

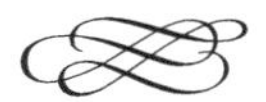

ELSA

The wagon rolled down the streets of Butte as the sun finally set and darkness fell over the city. Street lamps lit the cobble path, and all around them were the sounds of horseshoes clomping against the stones. A mist cloaked the air with a haze, and Elsa tightened the wrap around her shoulders.

"I didn't think we would travel during a storm," Jasper said. He moved closer to her, and while he looked as though he wanted to wrap his arm around her, he didn't. For a moment, she wondered how it would have felt if he had and how she would have reacted. Would it have shocked her so much she would have moved away from him? Or would she have leaned into him?

She wanted to believe it would have been the latter.

Although she knew deep down this had been her city, a place she had known, and a place she'd lived, it was more a stranger to her than Lone Hollow and Jasper had been when they first met after the accident. And as she looked around at the darkened streets, they felt hollow and cold like an unwelcoming party host who only allowed her into their party because they had to and not because they wanted to.

"Is anything ringing a bell?" Jasper asked.

"What do you mean?"

"Do you recognize anything? Like any of the streets or buildings?"

"No. Not yet." She tightened the wrap around her shoulders even more, and a chill wiggled down her spine. She blew out a breath. "Are we almost to the theater?"

"I think so. If I'd known the weather was going to be like this, I would have brought us some extra blankets."

"It's all right. I'm sure we will be dry and warm in no time." She glanced down at the crate near her feet; thankful Jasper had put extra hay in it for Sniffer to snuggle into during the ride.

"Don't worry about him," Jasper said, noticing her looking at the rabbit. "He's plenty warm in there under that hay."

"I know. He's just so tiny."

"And he'll be fine. Or she'll be fine."

"I'm just going to go with him until I know one way or another." She paused, chuckling to herself. "And even then, if I find out it's a she, I might still get it wrong."

"I'm sure she'll appreciate that." He laughed.

The two continued down the street until they rounded a corner, and a painted sign with the words Half Moon Theater came into view. Elsa sucked in a breath as she read the words over and over again. While none of them sparked any memories, she couldn't help but feel as though she'd seen them before. Like déjà vu, or whatever that French word was, she'd heard who knows how many times in her life.

"There it is," Jasper said. He pulled the horse to a stop in front of the door, and they both looked at the building. "Are you ready?" he asked.

"As ready as I'll ever be, I guess."

She heaved another sigh as he climbed out of the wagon,

helped her down, and grabbed the crate, tucking it under his arm as they both crossed the footpath and made their way to the door.

It opened as she reached for the doorknob, and an older gentleman dressed in a smart tuxedo stepped between the doorframe. His eyes widened.

"Miss Crestwood! I didn't know if I'd ever see you again. I'm so glad you are here."

"Thank you, Mr . . ." She cocked her head to the side as she couldn't place the man or his name.

"Mr. Thomas, Miss Crestwood."

"Mr. Thomas. Thank you. I'm sorry, but I'm having trouble remembering things right now."

"Oh, that's too bad. I'm sorry to hear that."

"Yes, well . . ." She let her voice trail off again, not knowing what else to say about her situation. Exactly how much did she want everyone to know? She still wasn't sure. "May I introduce Mr. Jasper Hemlock? I've been staying in his guest house, and he offered to bring me to Butte."

"Oh, that's nice of him." The two men shook hands, and as they let go of their handshake, Mr. Thomas nodded toward Elsa. "Your uncle is in his office. He's going to be so excited to see you."

"All right." She moved a few steps away from the doorman passing through the door and into the lobby of the theater before she hesitated and turned to face him. "And exactly where is his office?"

Mr. Thomas smiled, ducking his chin slightly. "It's down the hallway and the last door on the left. Your dressing room is the first door on the right."

She closed one eye, glancing up at the ceiling as she repeated the instructions. "Got it. Thank you."

After Mr. Thomas gave her another nod and pretended to tip a hat that really wasn't on his head, she headed down the hallway. Jasper followed close behind her, and as they neared the last door, her heart thumped.

She lifted her hand, and although she clenched it in a fist to knock, she hesitated.

"Is something the matter?" Jasper asked.

"I . . . I don't know if I can knock. What am I supposed to say?"

"Hello, would probably suffice after the last few weeks."

"No, I know that." Although amused at his joke, she held a little annoyance in her tone, and he chuckled even more at her response.

"Do you want me to handle it?" he asked.

She bit her lips and nodded, and without another word, he moved around her, getting between her and the door. Before she could say anything, he clenched his fist and knocked.

"Come in," a male's voice answered.

Jasper followed the command and twisted the doorknob, popping the door open.

"How may I help you?" the man asked.

"I think I might be able to help you." Jasper opened the door a little wider, and Elsa peeked around from behind him, moving into the doorframe.

The man sitting at the desk rose to his feet and removed his glasses, tossing them down on the desk.

"Elsa? Is it really you?" he asked.

"Yes."

He darted from around the back of the desk and rushed toward her, clutching her shoulders before drawing her into him for a hug. "Oh my. I'm so happy to see you. I didn't know where you went or what happened to you. Where did you go? What happened to you? You just left that night, and no one ever saw you again."

"I'm afraid your niece was in an accident, and there was damage to her . . . she doesn't have many memories of her life."

Jasper shoved both his hands into his pockets as he rocked back and forth from his toes to his heels.

The man looked between them and hugged Elsa once more. "Oh, my dear niece, I'm so sorry for what has happened to you. Does this mean . . . do you not remember me?"

Tears welled in her eyes as she wiggled away from him and shook her head. "No. I'm sorry. But I don't."

His lips thinned as he pressed them tight together and nodded. "I see. Well, I'm your uncle. My name is Clancy. I was your father's brother."

"Do you know where my parents are? Are they living in the city? Are they looking for me, too?"

"I'm afraid they are no longer with us. They were on a boat trip to Europe, and the boat sank on the way home."

"Sank?"

"Yes, I'm afraid so. You were only about ten or eleven, and that is when you came to live with me."

While Elsa hadn't known what to expect for the answers to her questions, the ones she got were the furthest from what she had in mind. She had hoped to hear the news that they were looking for her and would be delighted to see her. But now, that wasn't going to happen, and it almost felt as though she'd lost them all over again.

"Oh." She paused for a moment, biting her lip. "Do I . . . am I married? Or courting anyone?"

"No. Although there are a great many of men, wish you were their wife in this city." Uncle Clancy chuckled with his joke. "You are quite the popular woman in Butte. There would be a huge line if you ever wished to have a beau."

"So, I haven't wanted one?"

"Not that I could tell. You were more content with going home after the performances. You always preferred to be alone."

"Do you know why?"

"No, actually, I don't. It was just something you liked. I think you found comfort being alone."

It was odd to Elsa to hear these words. Only because in the last week or so since the accident, she had found more comfort in the company of Benjamin and Jasper. She hated being in the guesthouse all alone and had spent as much as she could get away with in their company instead.

"What is that?" Uncle Clancy asked, pointing toward the crate still tucked under one of Jasper's arms.

"It's my rabbit."

"Your what?" Clancy gaped at her, blinking several times.

"My rabbit. I'm going to keep it with me."

Her uncle continued to glance between her and the crate with his eyes wide. Then, as if to figure it pointless to argue, he shrugged. "Whatever you want, Elsa. I'm just happy you are home where you belong." He smiled a giant gin and stepped away from her as he snapped his fingers. "I should get Mrs. Meyers."

"Who?"

He held up his finger, wigging it before he hurried over to the door and poked his head back out into the hallway. "Mrs. Meyers! Mrs. Meyer's come here, please." His voice echoed down the hallway, and it wasn't but a moment later that a short, plump woman came into the office. Her mouth gaped open, and she gasped as she saw Elsa. She laid her hand on her chest and blinked.

"Mrs. Meyer's, our beloved Elsa has returned. Can you please tell Loraine we won't need her tonight? Then after that, get Elsa back to her dressing room and ready."

"Ready for what?" Jasper asked. His brow furrowed.

"Ready to perform, of course. The locals will be so happy she's returned. Loraine is a decent singer, but she's nothing like Elsa. I can't wait to tell them." He clapped his hands together and moved back over and around his desk, opening up a box sitting on the corner. He yanked out a cigar and lit it. Smoke billowed over his head.

"I don't think Elsa should perform tonight," Jasper said.

"Why not?"

"Because she's been through something traumatic. She didn't even know her name up until two days ago. She should be taken to her home where she can rest and settle back into a life and world she doesn't remember."

Uncle Clancy waved his hand. "That's ridiculous. Nothing will help Elsa more than getting back on that stage and singing. It might even do her good and help her regain her memories."

"I know you want to get her back on stage, so your customers are happy, but don't you think it's best to consider her health. I would think you would want your niece to be safe and to not force her into something she shouldn't do."

Uncle Clancy moved back around the desk, taking a few puffs on the cigar. More smoke billowed around his head, and he narrowed his eyes.

"Mrs. Meyers, can you take Elsa back to her dressing room?" As the woman approached Elsa, Elsa turned toward her.

"But what about Jasper?"

"Don't worry, Elsa." Uncle Clancy motioned for her to go with the woman. "There is a couch in the dressing room, and you can rest if you want. I'll send . . . Mr. Hemlock to find you in a few minutes. I just would like to have a chat with him first."

Elsa looked at Jasper, and he smiled and nodded. "It's all right. Go to your dressing room and rest for a bit. I'll be there shortly."

Although she wanted to stay, she did as the two men told her and followed Mrs. Meyers out of the office and down the hallway to the dressing room. As they reached the door, a man opened it from inside her room. Mrs. Meyer jumped back.

"Mr. Gilbert," she said, brushing her hand against her chest. "I didn't know you were here."

"Well, I heard the good news that Miss Crestwood has returned . . ." He motioned toward Elsa and reached out, laying his hand on her shoulder. "So good to have you back."

"Thank you."

"Mr. Bates wished for me to see Miss Crestwood to her dressing room." Mrs. Meyer said.

"I can do that for you."

Mrs. Meyer hesitated and looked between Elsa and Mr. Gilbert. She bit her lip, and after Mr. Gilbert cleared his throat —as though to tell her something without words—she finally nodded. "Very well. I'll see to my other chores until I'm needed."

As Mrs. Meyer made her way down the hallway, Mr. Gilbert opened the door a bit wider, motioning Elsa inside. "After you, Miss Crestwood."

THIRTEEN

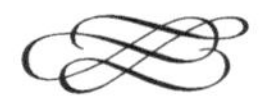

JASPER

Jasper set the rabbit crate down on the floor and watched as Elsa left the office and headed down the hallway. Nerves clenched in his stomach. He didn't care for the Half Moon Theater. This place was off to him. And Elsa's Uncle Clancy was off. He just didn't know what it was about the man that made him feel like it.

Clancy puffed on his cigar a few more times before removing it from his lip and glancing down at it.

"I want to thank you for bringing my niece home safe. I can't even imagine what would have happened to her if she'd fallen into the wrong hands."

"I don't understand what you mean."

"Well, you know, she could have been found by a man who knows who she is and would try to swindler her out of her money or something more . . . sinister."

A hint of annoyance flickered in Jasper's chest. "It's hard to swindle someone out of their money when they don't know who they are or that they have it."

"I guess you have a point."

The two men continued to stare at one another as though studying one another for any weakness they could pounce on.

Jasper couldn't take the silence anymore, and he cleared his throat. "What is Elsa's home address?"

"Why?" Clancy's eyes narrowed.

"So, I can take her home. That's where she should be. Home. Resting."

"But as I said, she's performing tonight. I will get her home after the show and after dinner with the customers."

"Dinner with the customers?"

"Yes. She always meets up with a few choice customers for dinner after the last show. They expect it."

"I don't care what they expect. She shouldn't be singing, and she definitely, shouldn't be having dinner with people throughout the hours of the night. She needs rest. She needs time to adjust. She just barely learned what her real name was."

Clancy smiled and snorted a laugh as he tucked his chin toward his chest and glanced down at the table. He took another puff on his cigar. The end lit up with a bright orange glow that burned at the paper and tobacco, leaving a clump of grey ashes. He tapped it on an ashtray, and the ashes fell off.

"I think I know what my niece needs. I've only raised her since she was ten years old. I know the type of person she is and how she handles things. You know, things about her that you couldn't possibly know only having spent so little time with her."

"I know more about her than you think I know."

Clancy's set his glare on Jasper, and his jaw clenched. "I highly doubt that."

"Why don't you ask her what she wants. Then after she tells you she wishes to go home, you'll listen to reason."

"It doesn't matter what she wants. She's a performer, and she knows this. She signed up for this when she wanted to be a singer and entertain people. And I bet you, after I remind her of this, she will agree with me."

"Why don't we ask her, then?"

"I'm not going to ask her." Clancy stuck the cigar in his mouth, holding it with his lips as he dug one hand into his pocket and yanked out a billfold. He flipped through the money, counting out a large chunk, and as he shoved the billfold back into his pocket with one hand, he outstretched the cash in the other.

"What's that?" Jasper asked, motioning toward the money.

"It's for your trouble and your time. I'm sure you need to get back to whatever tiny town you manage to make a living in, and I assume you will want to leave immediately."

"I don't want your money, and I'm not going anywhere until I see Elsa home safe."

"That's not your concern anymore."

Jasper didn't know if he could take the arrogance of this man another second. The last thing he needed was to get arrested in Butte for beating someone up or causing a fight. Not to mention, while he hadn't seen any goons hanging out around the office entrance, just the mere look of the man made Jasper's suspicions perk up. Surely, there was a man or two, or five, just waiting for a signal from their boss to escort Jasper outside—and not in a friendly manner.

If Jasper wanted to see Elsa or speak to her one last time, he would have to play it calm and calculate his next move.

"May I at least say goodbye to her?" He glanced down at the floor in front of him, staring at the crate with the rabbit inside. "And make sure her rabbit is put in her dressing room?"

Clancy's eyes narrowed, and he shoved the money back into his pocket. "I don't think that would be a good idea. I can have one of my men see to the . . . rabbit. I think it would be better if you just left Elsa to get back to her life again."

"I don't want to think I just left without saying goodbye."

"I can let her know your sentiment."

"It's still not the—"

"Mr. Hemlock, I didn't want to do this, but I'd hate to have you thrown out of my theater. It would be better for you just to take the hint and leave. The sooner, the better."

Jasper opened his mouth but shut it before he said a word. While he'd figured this would be the outcome to his questions to see Elsa again, he had hoped Clancy would surprise him and allow him to see her, even if it was for a few short minutes. His plans were sinking like a ship in the sea . . . and fast. He had to come up with another idea; he just didn't know what.

"Fine. I'll see myself out."

"It's for the best, and while I know you don't see it that way now, you will. She needs to get back to her own life." Clancy moved around Jasper and made his way to the door, opening it. "If you could do that immediately, that would be helpful. I need to check on Elsa and see if she needs anything."

A growl vibrated through Jasper's lips as he turned and headed through the door, veering in the opposite direction down the hallway toward the theater's lobby. His plans had all but failed, and he was not only out of options but out of ideas, and his heart thumped at the thought of not ever seeing Elsa again. He had to do something.

But what?

He hesitated for a moment in the lobby, glancing around at the chairs and tables. Customers would soon fill them all while they waited for the doormen to open the theater doors and allow them down to the seating near the stage. Although he'd never been to a show like this, he could almost hear them all chatting away about ridiculous topics such as the weather or perhaps banking or land purchases like rich people always talk about.

"Sir?" Mr. Thomas, the doorman, stood with his head cocked to one side. "Are you all right?"

"Yeah." Jasper nodded. His gaze moved off the doorman and unfocused on the floor for a moment. "I just . . . when are the show—"

"Psst!" a voice hissed behind him.

He spun around to face Mrs. Meyers. Her eyes were still wide, and she fidgeted with her hands.

"Mrs. Meyer?"

She waved her hands. "Shh. Keep your voice down." She glanced over his shoulder, pointing at Mr. Thomas. "Not a word, Jerry." The doorman nodded and turned his attention toward the door while she grabbed Jasper's arm and led him over to a dark corner of the lobby behind a tall piano that rested along the wall. "I need to talk to you."

Her voice was a mere whisper, and it wasn't just the tone of it that caught some concern in his chest, but also it was the way she was going out of her way not to get caught stopping and talking to him.

"What's going on, Mrs. Meyer?"

"Shh. I said, keep your voice down. Do you want them to hear you?"

"Who to hear me?"

"Mr. Bates or that man of his, Mr. Gilbert." She trembled as though a chill ran down her back, and she closed her eyes for a moment. "If they catch you or me here . . . they'd have both of our heads."

"What are you talking about?"

"You can't leave. Not without her. You've got to get her away from here."

"What do you mean I've got to get her away from here?" Jasper grabbed the woman's shoulder with his hand, squeezing it. His knees weakened, and his chest hollowed. All his breath was kicked out of it with the tone of Mrs. Meyer's words, and he struggled to inhale more.

"Mrs. Meyer!" a voice called out from down the hallway.

Both Mrs. Meyer and Jasper froze.

"That's Mr. Bates. He's calling for me." She turned to leave, and Jasper reached out, stopping her. "Wait. You can't just leave without telling me what is going on?"

"Wait for me in the alleyway behind the theater."

"What are—"

"Just wait for me in the alleyway. I will come for you." She wiggled from his grasp, and before he could agree or disagree, protesting that she tell him what was going on, Mrs. Meyer's trotted off down the hallway toward Elsa's dressing room. He didn't know what was going on, but gut instinct told him he wouldn't like it when he found out.

FOURTEEN

ELSA

Elsa moved around the dressing room, ignoring the man Mrs. Meyer called Mr. Gilbert as he stood near the couch and watched her. Neither of them said a word, and she wouldn't even look in his direction as she walked around. Dresses hung on several racks in the corner; their bright colors seemed to gleam in the light of the wall sconces. She studied not only each of the dresses but the sconces. A few flashes of memories fluttered in her mind of various times she'd worn a dress in particular. Like the blue one, with the satin material that felt so smooth and soft on her fingertips. She remembered wearing that one and remembered heading into a building one night. The faint memory that she hadn't wanted to be there toyed with her.

Had someone forced her?

"I didn't think we would see you again," Mr. Gilbert finally said. An odd smirk spread across his lips, and he shook his head as he let out a deep breath.

She wanted to ask him if that was a good or bad thing but decided it was best not to say a word.

"Where did you run off to?" he asked.

She shrugged. "I don't know where I was headed. But I ended up in Lone Hollow." A faint smile spread across her lips as she mentioned the town she'd come to love. She didn't want to admit that looking around at the dressing room not only hadn't brought back any memories, but it also had only made her long for the life she'd left in the tiny town even more.

"Huh. I've never heard of it." He leaned against the couch's armrest in the corner and folded his arms across his chest.

"It's a small town."

"Must be." Mr. Gilbert snorted a laugh, and he started pacing again for a moment before he spun and faced her. He pointed his finger at her. "And—"

The door to the dressing room opened, and Uncle Clancy came into the room carrying the rabbit crate. With an exhaled breath, she rushed over, taking the crate from him and setting it on the top of the vanity. The size of the crate pushed everything else on top of the vanity off to the side, and a perfume bottle teetered for a moment before it fell over and landed on its side. The glass clanked on the wood.

"Where is Jasper?" she asked Uncle Clancy, noticing Mrs. Meyer, who had entered the dressing room behind Elsa's uncle.

"He's gone."

"Gone?" Her head jerked, and her brow furrowed. "What do you mean gone?"

"He left."

"But he . . . didn't say goodbye. I thought he was going to say goodbye."

"Well, I guess he changed his mind."

"That doesn't seem like him." She moved toward the door, but Uncle Clancy stepped in front of her. "He's already gone. There is no point in going after him."

"But it just doesn't make sense."

Uncle Clancy heaved a deep breath, reaching for her shoulders as he exhaled. "I know it doesn't. But things don't always make sense anymore these days. However, the point of all of this is that you are finally home. And we must get you ready for the show tonight."

"The show tonight?"

"Of course. Your fans have missed you, and they will be overjoyed to see you on stage again."

Her heart thumped. It wasn't that she didn't know if she could sing or that she didn't know if she could sing in front of people. It was that she didn't know what was going on. She was in a room full of strangers, and although she had been told they were family, she couldn't help but feel as though there was a reason she left.

Why would she vanish?

Why did she leave?

"I didn't know I would have to perform tonight."

"Well, I mean . . . I suppose you don't have to. But it would be good for business, and it would be good for you."

Good for business.

She'd heard those words before.

Several times.

And looking upon Uncle Clancy's face as he said them, a few more memories sparked. He said that a lot to her, especially when she didn't want to do something like go out for dinner with specific customers after the show—usually men, and usually ones who made her skin crawl. Of course, she didn't remember any of them touching her, but they all made her uncomfortable.

Had that been why she left? Had she grown tired of Uncle Clancy using her?

"I want to go home."

"I understand, and I will take you home . . . after the show."

She stared at him for a moment as an itch crawled up the back of her neck. While she didn't know the exact reasons she'd left this theater the night they said she did, she was starting to realize that something was going on she didn't like. "Right after the show?"

"If that is what you want."

"It is."

Uncle Clancy clapped his hands together, then rubbed them. "Then that is what you shall have. But first, we need to get you ready for the show." He turned to Mrs. Meyer. "Get her ready, do her hair and make-up, and help her get dressed. Oh, the customers . . . they will be so pleased to hear the news of your return."

With the last of his words, he motioned Mr. Gilbert to follow him, and they left the room, leaving the two women alone. As soon as the door shut, Mrs. Meyer turned to Elsa, grabbing her shoulders.

"Why did you come back? Why didn't you stay away?"

Elsa sucked in a breath. "What are you talking about?"

"It's too much to tell you. Right now, we need to get you out of here." The woman turned toward the door, tugging on one of Elsa's arms to make her follow.

"What is going on?"

"There's no time to explain. That man you came here with is waiting for us in the alleyway." She tugged on Elsa again before she opened the door and checked down both sides of the hallway. "I think it's clear."

JASPER

After securing his gun from his wagon, Jasper trotted around to the alleyway behind the theater. His heart pounded, and he paced near the door. He didn't know how long he'd have to wait, and he fought with himself to keep his control. He wanted nothing more than to rush through the door, his gun blazing as he demanded answers.

He knew that would do more harm than good, though, so he paced.

It was all he could do.

Night settled in around him while he waited, and as he glanced around, a figure emerged from the darkness, pointing a gun at him. The steel glinted in the moonlight.

"Who are you?" Jasper asked.

The man cocked his head to the side, and a half-smirk spread through his lips. "Does it matter?"

"I suppose it doesn't."

Is this what Mrs. Meyer had meant, he thought to himself. *Had the woman sent him around the theater so this man could come and take him out?*

"I believe my boss told you to leave," the man said.

"He did. But I chose not to listen."

"I can see that." The man paused, exhaling a sigh. "You know, I gotta say, a part of me wonders why."

"I'm just trying to make sure Elsa is safe."

"So, that's what it's about then? Miss Crestwood?" A slight chuckle vibrated through the man's chest. "I thought my boss told you not to worry about her."

"He did."

"So why are you here?"

"Because I didn't care for his tone when he told me."

"You think he'd hurt his own niece?"

"I'm not sure. But something made her run away from here that night she left, and I'm not leaving until I find out what happened and what is going on."

The man opened his mouth, but before he could utter a word, the backdoor of the theater opened, and Mrs. Meyer and Elsa stepped outside.

"Elsa, wait!" Jasper tried to warn them, but before they knew what was going on, the man rushed over behind them and slammed the door, shutting them off from escape. He pointed the gun at all three of them.

"Well, well. Mrs. Meyer. I would never have guessed you would be so disloyal to your boss."

"And I never would have guessed he would have ordered the murder of his own niece."

Jasper moved around to Elsa and grabbed the poor woman, shifting Mrs. Meyer behind them both as he pulled his gun from his holster. He pointed it at the man.

"I should have figured you'd be armed," the man said.

"Yeah. You should have."

"And you should have figured that I wouldn't be alone."

With the man's words, another gun clicked in the darkness and a second man stepped out from behind them. Elsa gasped, and she inched herself closer to Jasper.

"You're outnumbered, Mr. Hemlock," Mr. Bates said. "Put down your gun."

"You think I either care about being outnumbered or that I haven't been in this situation before?"

Mr. Bates' eyes narrowed, and one of them twitched. "Fine. Put it down, or I'll shoot her right here in this alleyway."

"You shoot her, and I'll shoot you."

"Not before I get you," the man said.

Jasper's gaze darted from Mr. Bates to the man, then back to Mr. Bates. He didn't want to admit that being outnumbered was a problem. Sure, he was a quick enough draw he could get the jump on a man but getting the jump on two of them before either could fire their weapon was a stretch.

No matter the odds, however, he wasn't going to back down.

One would get him, but not before he got one of them first and perhaps the second. Even if he didn't make it, Elsa would have a chance.

He glanced over his shoulder, dropping his voice to a whisper. "Get behind me."

Her brow furrowed, and although she started to follow his order, she hesitated and turned toward her uncle.

"What are you doing?" he asked.

She ignored him, squaring her shoulders at Mr. Bates. "Why are you doing this? I thought you were my family. My only family." Her voice cracked.

Mr. Bates stared at her for a moment, then snorted. "Plans change, Elsa."

"I don't understand."

"My brother's house. My brother's money. My brother's stocks. My brother's business holdings. They were all supposed to be mine when he died. And I thought they were. It turns out they aren't."

"I don't understand."

"I didn't want to believe that it was true. Not when the lawyer visited me. Not when he told me of the provisions in the trust. I knew everything was locked up until you reached twenty years old. I just didn't know how locked up they were. I was supposed to get it all. Not you. Everything wasn't supposed to go to a woman. Especially one who has a fortune all her own, and a fortune she wouldn't have if it weren't because of me. Your house. Your stardom. The love from the crowd. All the diamonds in your jewelry box. All the money that is in your bank. It's all because of me, and it should be mine."

"So, that's what this is about? Money?" Jasper tried to move between them again, but Elsa shifted around him, inching closer to Mr. Bates. "You want her dead so that you can collect on her parent's fortune and hers?"

"This matter doesn't concern you. It's between my niece and me." Mr. Bates swallowed, adjusted his stance, and pointed the gun at her head.

~

ELSA

"Don't test me. I'll do it."

Elsa stared down the barrel of the gun and blinked. Although fuzzy, memories started to flicker inside her mind.

"I remember leaving that night. I was attacked in my dressing room." She glanced over at Mr. Gilbert. "It was you." She then looked back at her uncle. "You ordered him to do it. And when I found out, I fled. I didn't tell anyone."

"You have ruined everything."

Everyone stood in silence in the middle of the alleyway. Mrs. Meyers cowered behind Elsa and Jasper while they faced Uncle Clancy and Mr. Gilbert. While Uncle Clancy had his gun trained on her, Jasper had his on her uncle, and Mr. Gilbert had his on Jasper. It was a standoff she didn't like and a standoff where she feared no one would come out a winner. Jasper had the least chance, and her heart thumped with the thought of something happening to him.

"If I give you everything you want, will you let us go?" she asked.

"Don't do that," Jasper said.

"This doesn't concern you!" Uncle Clancy pointed the gun toward Jasper as he shouted, and Elsa sucked in a breath. She moved between the two men, but Jasper blocked her and pointed his gun at her uncle.

"I'm not going to let you near her," Jasper said.

The two men stared at one another, and as Uncle Clancy opened his mouth, a gunshot rang out behind them. Everyone spun to see the Sheriff and a few of his men running down the alleyway. Mr. Gilbert fled into the backdoor of the theater, and after watching his only backup leave, Uncle Clancy pointed the gun back toward Elsa.

"Another week, and I could have pronounced you dead. Another week and I could have had it all. You've always ruined everything. Always."

He pulled the trigger, and as the gun fired, Jasper shoved her to the side and lunged for Uncle Clancy. Their bodies collided, and they fell to the ground. Jasper struggled to gain the upper hand with only one arm, but after he punched her uncle several times, her uncle lay unconscious on the ground. His face was cut and bleeding.

Regaining her balance, she rushed over to Jasper, helping him stand. "Are you all right?" she asked.

"Yeah. Are you?"

"Yes."

He wrapped his arm around her, and they clutched each other, holding on as tight as they both could while the Sheriff and his man picked Uncle Clancy up off the ground. The man, although groggy, woke up and fought with them before they were able to bind him properly.

"Thank you for your help, Sheriff. You got here just in time."

"It's my pleasure."

"How did you know there was trouble?" Elsa asked him.

The sheriff tipped his hat. "The doorman, Mr. Thomas. He came and fetched me, told me everything that was going on. I'm sorry we couldn't piece the whole thing together after you were first attacked, Miss Crestwood."

"It's all right. It turned out for the best anyway."

His head jerked slightly with her answer, and his brow furrowed as though he was confused. He shook his head, then gave her a half-smile as he tipped his hat again. "If you say so, ma'am. I best get Mr. Bates off to jail. I'll file the charges in the morning and be by your house in the afternoon to get your statements."

"Thank you."

As the sheriff made his way over to Uncle Clancy, Jasper hugged her again, drawing her away from her uncle to shield her from watching him walk away. Although she wanted to give her uncle one last look, she didn't. Instead, she melted in Jasper's arms, leaning her body against his chest.

"May I ask you something," he said as though he wanted to distract her more.

"What?"

"Why did you tell the sheriff it was the best that he didn't catch your uncle before? If he had, you wouldn't have had to go through all of this."

"I know. But if he had, I never would have left Butte and gotten into the accident."

"You say that like it's a good thing."

"It is. It brought me to you."

He pressed his lips into hers, kissing her for a moment, and as he pulled away, he rested his forehead on hers, lowering his voice to a whisper. "Now what?"

"Now . . . we go home . . . home to Lone Hollow."

FIFTEEN

ELSA

Elsa looked down at all the dresses laid out on the bed, and a slight groan vibrated through her chest. None of them was right. None of them were perfect.

None of them was the one.

"It's just not what I had in mind," she said aloud to herself, ignoring how doing so made her feel a little silly. "None of them will work. None. I might as well get married in a burlap sack."

She spun away from the bed, catching sight of her reflection in the mirror above the vanity. She only had a little time to get ready before Benjamin would be here to escort her to the barn. It had been the perfect location for them to get married, and while she already had the perfect hairstyle and the perfect bunch of wildflowers for the bouquet, now all she needed was the perfect dress.

And it was the one thing she didn't have.

"What am I supposed to do?" she asked her reflection.

A knock rapped on the door, and as she opened it, Benjamin popped his head inside. "Are you ready?"

She rolled her eyes and growled. "Hardly. None of the dresses will work."

"What do you mean?" Benjamin's brow furrowed, and she opened the door a little more, letting him inside the room.

She pointed toward the bed, raising her voice before slapping her arm down by her side. "I don't want to wear any of them."

"Are you sure none of them will work?"

"Yes, I'm sure. None of them are . . . they just aren't right."

He smiled at her, and it was then she noticed he had something hidden behind his back.

"What do you have?"

"Well . . ." He shifted his hands from behind him and held out something folded in a piece of material in his hands. "I thought maybe you would like to try it on. Maybe you would wear it when you married Jasper."

"What is it?" She flipped open the top layer of the material, exposing a folded cream-colored dress with a layer of beautiful lace.

"It was Emma's, my wife. She wore it when we got married. She had saved it, thinking if we ever had a daughter . . ." He tucked his chin, chuckling. "Of course, when Jasper was born, she then changed her thought of if she ever had a daughter-in-law, perhaps that young lady might want to wear it. If she didn't have her own mother's dress, that is."

Elsa said nothing as she finished unwrapping the dress and laid it down on the bed, fanning the cotton and lace skirt. She fought tears as her gaze traced over the lace pattern and memorized all the buttons up the sleeves and down the front.

"It's . . ."

"I know it's old. If you'd rather not wear—"

"No. Benjamin, I was going to say it's perfect. It's exactly what I want to wear. It's everything that all these other dresses aren't. I'd be so honored to wear it. Truly, I would."

The old man clammed up and nodded as his eyes filled with tears. "Well, I think she would have been honored too."

"Just let me change, and I'll be ready. All right?"

"Sounds good. I'll be waiting just outside."

As he hurried back through the door, she slipped out of her robe and unbuttoned all the buttons down the front before she grabbed the dress and stepped inside the skirt. She slid it up over her hips and glided her arms down the sleeves. Her heart pounded as she fastened every last button from the middle of the bodice up to her neck. The dress fit as though made for her, and with one last look in the mirror, she finally saw the reflection she'd wanted to see.

"Now, it's perfect," she whispered.

She fought her tears as she made her way to the door, but as she opened it and saw Benjamin start crying when he saw her, the dam broke, and the tears she'd been fighting streamed down her cheeks.

"It looks stunning on you. Just as it did on her."

"Thank you for letting me wear it."

"You're most welcome." He held out his arm for me to take. "I think it's about time we get you and Jasper hitched, don't you think?"

She laughed and hooked her arm through his. "Why, yes, I do."

Entering the barn had felt real and yet like a dream all at the same time, and as Elsa walked down the aisle toward Jasper, she couldn't help but feel as though nothing else in the world mattered but him.

"You look beautiful," he said to her as she took his arm.

Like the earth beneath their feet, his tranquil nature kept everything surrounding him together in peace and harmony. Jasper was her rock, her strength. He held the very key that allowed her to dream but kept her feet on the ground at the same time. He was her home. Her life. And she couldn't believe she'd been so lucky as to find him.

There had been a few times in her life where she had prayed

for such a love and such a man. Never thinking she would find him, she'd fallen into the trap of deciding her hopes were nothing more than a misconception on her part, believing that such love didn't exist, or her prayers would go unanswered.

And she was happy to now know she had been so wrong.

She was about to marry the man who was everything she'd ever hoped and prayed for.

THE END

DID YOU READ THEM ALL?

Five men looking for love . . .

Five women with different ideas . . .

One small town where they all will either live happily ever after or leave with shattered dreams.

CHECK OUT THE SERIES ON AMAZON! AND PICK UP THE ONES YOU MAY HAVE MISSED TODAY!

WAGON TRAIN WOMEN

Five women headed out West to make new lives on the Frontier find hope and love in the arms of five men. Their adventures may be different, but their bond is the same as they embark on the journey together in the same wagon train.

CHECK OUT THE SERIES ON AMAZON!

Turn the page for a sneak peek at book one, Her Wagon Train Husband.

ONE

ABBY

Everyone loves adventure.

Well, almost everyone.

Abby had to correct herself on that point. Her parents didn't like adventure much. Neither did her three older sisters. They liked being home. They liked being in a place they knew. They didn't enjoy the thrill of the unknown or the sense that the world could open up right under their feet.

Of course, that wasn't an appealing thought. For surely that would mean death. And Abby didn't like the idea of that. She just liked the adventure.

Yeah, she thought to herself. I don't like that.

Abby heaved a deep sigh as she walked along the path around the lake. It was a favorite pastime for her and one she enjoyed nearly every day. Well, every day that her parents and sister's stayed in their country home. When they were in the city . . . well, that was another story. She would often sneak out of the house and head to the park. Even if she had to be careful about being seen, she would still try to get in a little walk in the trees and sunshine. Wasn't that what Spring and Summer were for? Perhaps even Autumn? Winter surely not, although she couldn't complain too much about those months. For she loved the snow too and would enjoy it until her fingers and nose turned red, and her skin hurt.

Something about nature called to her like a mother calls to a child when they want them to come home or to the table to sit down and share a meal. She loved everything about it. The smell of the air, the sound of the birds, and the leaves rustling in the breeze. The feel of the sunshine upon her skin and how it felt as though her body tried to soak it all in like a rag soaks up water.

The outdoors made her feel alive.

Much like the sense of adventure did.

And the two, she thought, went hand in hand.

"Aammeelliiaa!" She heard a woman's voice call out in the distance. Her name was long and drawn out and sounded as though the woman—her mother—calling had her hands up against the sides of her mouth.

Her heart thumped. She couldn't be caught coming from the direction of the lake, and yet, there would be no chance to sneak around to the other side of the stables without being seen. Her mother called for her several more times, and as she tried to round the stables, appearing as though she came from a different direction, she heard her mother's foot stomp on the front port.

"Abby Lynn Jacobson! And just where have you been?" Her mother raised her hand as if to stop her from answering. "Don't even tell me you were walking around that lake all by yourself."

"All right." Abby squared her shoulders. "I don't tell you that."

Her mother's eyes narrowed, and she pointed her finger in Abby's face. "You listen to me, young lady; you will not go flittering off again. Do you understand me? You have far too many responsibilities in this house to do anything other than what you're supposed to be doing."

"But sewing and cooking and cleaning are just so boring. I want to be outside."

"Outside is no place for a woman unless they are out there to hang laundry on the line or gardening. Both of which you need to be doing too." Her mother continued to wave her hands around the outside of the house, pointing toward the laundry line and the fenced garden around the back of the house. Clothes already hung on the line, and they moved in the breeze. "Your sisters certainly don't spend any time fooling around outside."

"That's because my sisters are married and have husbands to look after."

"And you will have one too. Sooner than later, now that your father has made it official."

"What do you mean?" Abby jerked her head, and her brow furrowed.

"Mr. Herbert Miller is on his way over to the house this afternoon."

"Why?" Although she asked, she wasn't sure she wanted the answer, nor did she believe she would like it.

Her mother shook her head and rolled her eyes. "To finalize the agreement and plans to marry you and take care of you, of course."

Abby sucked in a breath and spit went down the wrong pipe. She choked and sputtered, coughing several times while she gasped. "I . . . I . . ." She coughed a few more times and held out her hand until she regained composure. "I don't want to marry him."

"That's not for you to decide. He comes from a well-to-do family and intends to provide a good life for you. Not to mention we could use the money." Her mother clasped her hands together and fidgeted with her fingers as she glanced around the home. It was still in good shape for its age, but even

Abby had seen some of the repairs it needed, and she knew her parents couldn't afford it. "I dare say he's the richest young man out of all your sister's husbands. You will have a better life than any of them."

"And you think I care about that?"

"You should. It's well known around St. Louis that the Millers have the means. There are mothers and fathers all over the city who would love to have him for a son-in-law. You're going to have quite the life, young lady."

"But is it quite the life if it's a life I don't want?"

"How can you not want it? A husband. A nice home. Children. It's all you've wanted."

"No, it's all you've wanted. And it's all my sisters have wanted."

"Oh, spare me talk of your dreams of adventure." She rolled her eyes again and wiggled her finger at her daughter. "There is plenty of adventure in being married and having children. Trust me."

"That's not the kind of adventure I want, Mother."

"It doesn't matter what you want, Abby. Your purpose in life and in this family is to marry and have children. If you're lucky, which it looks like you are, you will marry a nice man with means. You should be happy. You could have ended up like Mirabel Pickens." Mother brushed her fingers across her forehead. "Lord only knows what her parents were thinking marrying her off to that horrible Mr. Stansbury on the edge of town. He's at least twice her age and hasn't two pennies to rub together. Of course, he acts like he does, but honestly, I think the Pickens family gives them money." Mother fanned her face with her hand. "Now, go upstairs and change your dress. Fix your hair too. He'll be here within the hour."

Before Abby could protest any further, her mother spun on her heel and marched back across the porch and into the back door of the kitchen. Abby stood on the porch. Part of her was too stunned for words, yet the other part wasn't shocked at all. She always knew this day was coming. It just had come a little sooner than she thought it would, and although she had thought of a few excuses or reasons she could give to put it off, with Herbert on his way to the house, she didn't know if any of them would work.

Scratch that.

She knew none of them would work.

Her parents had their eyes set on the young Mr. Miller for a while, and there wasn't any reasoning they would listen to that would change their minds.

It wasn't that Herbert—or Hewy as he once told her she could call him—was a dreadful young man. He wasn't exactly what she would call the type of man she would hope to marry, but he was nice. He was taller than most men his age and skinner, and he wore thick glasses that always seemed to slip down his nose as he talked. He was constantly pushing them back up, and there were times Abby wondered if he ever would buy a pair that fit better or if he enjoyed the fact they were a size too big. Like had it become a habit for him and one he liked.

She remembered how distracting it had been at the Christmas dance last December that her parent's friends hosted at their house. Every few steps, he would take his hand off her waist to push them back up his nose, and he would even miss a step here and there, throwing them both off balance because he had to lead. He'd even stepped on her foot once or twice.

Her toe throbbed for days after that party.

No. She simply could not marry him. She just couldn't.

If her mother wouldn't see reason, perhaps her pa would.

She marched across the porch and into the house, making her way toward his office and knocking on the door.

"Come in," her pa said from the other side, and as she

opened it and moved into the room, he glanced up from his desk and smiled. "Good afternoon, Abby."

"Well, it's an afternoon, but I'm not sure it's a good one."

He cocked one eyebrow and threw the pencil in his hand down onto a stack of papers on the desk. "What has your mother done now?"

"She's informed me that Mr. Herbert Miller is on his way to the house to finalize an agreement for my hand in marriage." She paused for a moment but then continued before her father could say a word. "Father, I know you aren't going to accept it. Right?"

"And what makes you say that?" He glanced down at the papers on his desk as he blew out a breath.

She knew where this conversation was headed. She'd seen this reaction in him she didn't know how many times in her life. When faced with a question that Pa didn't want to answer, he used work as his excuse to ask whoever was asking him what he didn't want to face to leave. She wasn't about to let him do it today.

"I don't care what you have on that desk that is so important, Pa, but quite frankly, I don't care. This is important. This is my future. I don't want to marry Herbert Miller. I don't love him. You've got to put a stop to this."

He reached up and rubbed his fingers into his temples. "What is it that you want me to say, Abby? I don't have time for this."

"I want you to say no and tell him that I'm not ready to marry and that you don't give him your blessing."

"You know I can't say that, young lady."

"For heaven's sakes, why not?"

"Because we've already agreed, and he's already paid off our debts."

"He's done what?" She didn't mean to shout, but she did anyway, and the look on her father's face as the loudness in her tone blared in his ears told her she should have given a second thought before letting her volume raise.

"Don't take that tone with me, young lady."

"I'm sorry, Pa. I didn't mean to. It's just that . . . I don't want to marry Herbert Miller."

"And I don't understand why you don't. He comes from a good family—"

"And he wants to provide me with a good life. I know." She threw her hands up in the air and paced in front of her father's desk. "Mother already told me all those things. But they don't matter. It doesn't matter how good his family is or what he wants to provide for me. I don't want to be like my sisters. You know this. You've always known this."

"Don't tell me you still have all those silly notions of adventure stuck in your head."

"They aren't silly."

"But they are!" He slapped his hand down on his desk. The force was so great that it rattled the oil lamp sitting on the edge, and the flame flickered. Abby flinched, and she stared at her pa, blinking.

Of course, she'd seen her father angry a time or two growing up. She didn't think there was a child alive who didn't see their parents in a fit at least once. It was what adults did.

But while she knew he could get that angry, she didn't expect to see it. At least not today. Not over this.

He fetched an envelope, opened it, and yanked out the money tucked inside. He threw it down on the table. "Do you see this? This is what will save this family. You are what will save this family. Abby, it's time you grow up and stop wasting your time and thoughts on silly things. You're not a child anymore. You're a woman. It's time for you to marry and take care of a husband and children. I know you have never talked about wanting those things, but I thought perhaps the older you became . . ."

"Well, you thought wrong." She folded her arms across her chest.

"Perhaps I did. But that doesn't change the fact that we will make the wedding plans when this young man comes over this afternoon."

"Pa, please, no. Don't make me do this."

He held up his hands. "I'm sorry, Abby, but I've already made my decision, and the deal is done. It's what I had to do to save this house and my family. And it was the best thing I could have done for you." He moved to the office door, opening it before he paused in the frame. "Now, if you'll excuse me, I must see to the rest of my work before this young man arrives."

"Pa?"

"Abby, this conversation is finished."

Tears welled in her eyes, and although she tried to blink them away, she couldn't, and they soon found themselves spilling over and streaming down her cheeks. She shook her head as she watched him leave the office. While she knew there had been a chance he wouldn't listen to her, she hoped he might.

And now that hope was gone, leaving her with only a sense of desperation.

What could she do? She couldn't marry Herbert. She just couldn't. She would rather run away than marry him.

Run away.

That was what she would do.

That was the answer.

If she wanted adventure when no one would give it to her, well then, she would simply take it for herself.

All she needed was to pack some clothes and get her hands on some money.

Money.

She glanced over her shoulder toward the pile of cash Pa had yanked out of the envelope. She didn't know how much was there, but it looked enough. Or she should say it looked like enough to get her where she wanted to go. It was hers after all, wasn't it? If she was the one sold like a farm animal?

She moved over to the desk, staring down at the paper bills.

She didn't have to take it all. She could leave some of it for her parents.

Never mind, she thought. *I'm taking every last dollar.*

TWO

WILLIAM

"Do you have room for my horse?"

William's eyes fluttered with the booming voice that filtered into the barn from the stalls and walkway below. He rolled over, and several stalks of hay poked his back through his shirt. He hated sleeping in the hayloft of a barn, but it was safer than sleeping in a stall. Not only could a horse step on him, or worse, lay down on him in a stall, but there was a better chance he would get caught if he was down there instead of up in the hayloft.

And he couldn't get caught.

Not unless he wanted to go to jail.

Which he didn't.

"Yeah. Just take the last stall on the left, Mr. Russell. Are you boarding for the day?" another voice asked.

"I'll be back for him around dawn. That's when we leave to take another trip to Oregon. I gots me a pocket full of money, and I want to have fun spending it."

William's ears perked up with the word money, and he rolled over again, scooting on his stomach toward the edge of the loft so he could look down upon the man. He couldn't glimpse the man's face looking down on the top of his hat, but the man was dressed in all black from his hat to his chaps. He watched as the man led his buckskin horse down the walkway into the stall and untacked it before throwing the saddle on the rack and hooking the bridle on the horn. He fed and watered the animal, then strode back toward the door. The rowels of his spurs clanked and rattled with each of his steps.

William knew he needed to get out of the barn before the stable master found him. He didn't know the price he would have to pay if caught sleeping in the hayloft, but he wasn't about to find out. He rolled up onto his knees, folding his blanket before shoving it in his bag and brushing the last crumbs of the stale loaf of bread he had for dinner, so they scattered in the hay.

Looking over the edge of the loft, he glanced around, and after making sure no one would see him, he scaled down the ladder, jumping off the last rung before he slung his bag over his shoulder and darted out the back door of the barn.

~

William hadn't ever been to Independence, Missouri before. He'd only heard about it in his brother's stories. They used to talk about coming here as young boys when they dreamed. It was known as the Queen City of the Trails. The starting point where those seeking to travel out west to the frontier started their journey. He hadn't known what to expect from this strange little city, but such didn't matter. All that did was that somehow, he found his way out of it.

And preferably by wagon on a wagon train headed to Oregon or California.

He wasn't picky about where he would go. He just needed to

get as far away from Missouri as possible and by any means he could.

Even if he had to work for it.

He trotted down the different alleyways between the buildings, staying off the main streets as he veered through town. He rounded the corner onto another street, and as he did, he came face to face with a small café. Scents of eggs, bacon, sausage, and potatoes wafted in the air, and his stomach growled as though to tell him it wanted everything the nose could smell. His mouth watered too, and he closed his eyes, imagining how it all tasted—which he was sure was delicious.

He hadn't eaten anything since finding that loaf of old bread in the garbage outside of the bakery yesterday morning, and while he had planned to go back there to check for more, the thought of stale, butterless bread was no match for the smell of a hot breakfast.

Opening his eyes, he glanced down at the ground. He didn't want more stale bread any more than he wanted to dig out his own eyes, but of course, there was one big problem. How to get it? Getting the bread was easy, but with empty pockets and not a nickel to his name, the hot breakfast was nothing short of impossible.

He heaved a deep sigh and hunched his shoulders as he kicked at a rock and watched it roll several inches. Admitting defeat was never easy, and this morning with a grumbling stomach was no exception.

Still, facts were facts. He didn't have the money, so bread it was.

He continued down the street, barely looking up as he passed the café. He didn't want to see the food any more than he wanted to smell it, but as he passed, he glanced out of the corner of his eye. A young couple was sitting at a table outside, chatting to one another. Distracted with their conversation, they didn't even look at William as he passed. Hesitation spurred through him, and he slowed down, watching as the man scooted his chair toward the woman, and they huddled their faces close to one another.

"And so, I told him, Mr. Dexter, I just can't marry your daughter because I'm in love with someone else," the man said.

"Oh, and just who might that be?" the woman asked.

The man scooted his chair even closer and grabbed her hands. "Why, you, my darling." While the woman ducked her chin, her face turned a bright shade of red, and she removed her handkerchief from her handbag, brushing her other hand along her chest. William wanted to retch at the sight of their love and affection for one another, but with an empty stomach, nothing would have come up. Not to mention, he would have drawn unwanted attention from what he was about to do.

He just needed to wait for the perfect moment . . .

Just as he had hoped, the man, so overcome with love, shoved his plate aside and out of his way. William lunged over the small fence separating the dining area from the sidewalk and grabbed the plate. The woman screamed, but as the man spun in his chair, William took off down the street with the plate tucked tight into his body so none of the food would spill.

~

William continued down the street and around another building, hiding behind several wooden crates stacked against the brick wall. He pressed his back against the bricks and glanced down both directions of the alleyway before sliding down to the ground and tucking his legs up until he was blocked from sight.

His lungs heaved, and he closed his eyes. "Lord. Please forgive me for stealing this food. I know it's wrong, and I have sinned. I hate to eat it, but . . . I'm starving. I pray for my forgiveness. In Jesus' name. Amen."

Although the first bite tasted like a little bit of heaven, the guilt gave it an unpleasant aftertaste. It was one he didn't like, but he also knew that he didn't know when he would see food again without stealing. He wanted to curse himself just as much as he wanted to curse his brother for putting him into this mess. And yet, he also knew that doing either of those wouldn't make the situation better.

Nothing would make it better.

Well, clearing his name would.

But knowing the solution and putting it into play were two different things. Pinkertons weren't about hearing reason. They just saw the words as excuses. The guilty are always trying to get out of punishment for their crimes, they would say, and no matter what he told them, they would only say it to him.

They wouldn't believe him.

Nor would they even give him the chance to explain.

He shoveled the last few bites of eggs into his mouth, both wanting to chew them slowly to savor them and also gobble them down so he could flee before anyone caught him. Once he had licked it clean, he tossed the plate aside, and another hint of guilt prickled in his chest as the bone white china smacked against the dirt with a thud sound. He wanted to return the plate to the café, and yet he knew that it would be foolish to do so.

Perhaps I can leave it outside the door tonight after dark, he thought. Do at least one good thing today, even if it's not much of one.

It would be the right thing to do.

He could almost hear his mama talking to him from Heaven above, telling him what he needed to do. Or course, that was nothing new. He listened to her daily, always on his case about one thing or another he did. Lord, she would roll over in her grave if she saw him now. He was glad she passed on so she wouldn't have to see the utter failure he'd become. As much as he hated to think that, he did, and it was just another thing to hate his brother for.

He heaved a deep sigh and slipped his hand into his pants pocket, pulling out a folded piece of paper. It was yellower than it had been months ago, and the edges were tearing from all the time spent in his pocket, and all the times he pulled it out, looked at it, and stuck it back in. It wasn't that looking at it gave him hope or comfort. It was just the opposite, actually. The paper only brought him fear, pain, and anger, and although he wanted to throw it away every second of every day, he also wanted to keep it. He didn't know why.

Perhaps it was the reminder he needed.

Or perhaps he was nothing but an utter fool.

He didn't know which.

But as he opened it and looked down upon the words 'WANTED' and a drawn picture of his face with his name below written in black ink, all the feelings came flooding back.

He was a wanted man.

And it was all his brother's fault.

To my sister
Michelle Renee Horning

April 3, 1971 - January 8, 2022
You will be forever missed. I don't know how I'm going to do this thing called life without you.

London James is a pen name for Angela Christina Archer. She lives on a ranch with her husband, two daughters, and many farm animals. She was born and raised in Nevada and grew up riding and showing horses. While she doesn't show anymore, she still loves to trail ride.

From a young age, she always wanted to write a novel. However, every time the desire flickered, she shoved the thought from my mind until one morning in 2009, she awoke with the determination to follow her dream.

www.authorlondonjames.com

Join my mailing list for news on releases, discounted sales, and exclusive member-only benefits!

Cover Design by Angela Archer, Long Valley Designs

Published in the United States of America by:

Long Valley Press
Newcastle, Oklahoma
www.longvalleypress.com

Made in the USA
Middletown, DE
14 April 2023

28867345R00090